*The Forest of Forgotten time*

*By Michele E. Northwood*

© 2024

Copyright© 2023 by Michele E. Northwood

This book is a work of fiction. Apart from known historical places, all characters and incidents are the product of the author's imagination and are fictitious.

All rights reserved. No part of this book may be reproduced or transmitted in any form or by any means, electronically or mechanically, including photocopying, recording or by any information storage and retrieval system, without the author's permission.

Cover Art by Get Covers.com

Book formatting by Randy V. Perez

**An ode to all non-British readers**

This poem is to apologise/apologize

I do not wish to offend your eyes,

But I'm a Brit and you may think

My spelling's completely on the blink (fritz).

My sombre/somber poem's for you to see,

You do not write the same as me.

You use a `z´ when I use `s´

In cosy/cozy and idealised/idealized - I guess...

I add a `u´ when you do not,

In honour/honor and colour/color (It happens a lot!)

Ambience/ambiance and travelling/traveling

Our difference in spelling is a curious thing!

So as you manoeuvre/maneuver through this book,

And at these differences, you look,

Mistakes for you are not for me.

(It's how I was taught, you see).

I need to emphasise/emphasize this well...

Before you assume I cannot spell!

I hope you'll enjoy this book you've bought.

and not give these differences another thought. Kind regards, Michele xx

**Chapters**

Chapter One.

Chapter Two.

Chapter three.

Chapter Four.

Chapter Five.

## Chapter One

Miles was the first to spy the young Indian man standing in the arrivals hall. A piece of torn, jagged cardboard hung limply in one hand, his other cupped the remains of a cigarette. His eyes were hidden behind mirrored sunglasses, yet his posture radiated fear and discomfort. His right leg jutted forward, and his heel tapped the floor in a constant, impatient rhythm.

Miles wondered if the slim young man was high on something.

Scrawled across the tattered cardboard were two names. He recognised his, but the other was way off the mark.

'I think that's our man,' Geoff said. He strode toward the individual with his right hand outstretched.

'That's just great!' Pint-sized Elizabeth snapped, dragging her heavy suitcase behind her and hitching up a bulky holdall. 'Typical. They've written both of your names on the card. Where's mine? Huh? Am I less important or something?'

Miles tried to hide his smile. His childhood friend had always been the same: feisty and ready for confrontation at the slightest inclination. He blamed her slight frame of five feet three inches for her combative attitude. She reminded him of a Yorkshire terrier. Tiny in frame, but ready to take on a Rottweiler and fight until the bitter end.

He zoned back in, while she continued complaining about her missing name.

'Of course, you're not less important. It's not a big piece of card, that's all. Maybe they ran out of space.' Miles wasn't sure his answer pacified her, but at least he had tried to limit her explosive outburst.

A deep frown furrowed her forehead. 'Oh, come on! You're telling me they couldn't write "Liz"? It's three measly letters!'

Miles grinned at his spirited best friend before turning his gaze toward the young Indian again. He assessed him a second time. His hair needed cutting. His clothes were clean, yet tatty around the cuffs of his shirt and the hems of his thin trousers. He was tall, thin-framed, with rounded shoulders that somehow gave him a servile demeanour. Miles wondered if he were there under duress. He appeared to want nothing more than to leave.

The distracted Indian jumped to attention when Geoff's right hand went to grab his cigarette-holding digits. He threw the cigarette to the ground as Geoff grasped his hand and pumped it up and down.

'Hi! My name is Geoff, and these are Miles and Liz.' He pointed to the cardboard. 'That's us!'

The young Indian man graced them with a weak smile. He pulled back his shoulders and shook his thick fringe out of his face.

'Hello,' he said, with a strong Indian twang. He gave a slight bow. 'My name is Amargeet. Please, follow me.'

Miles and Geoff fell in step behind him. Liz brought up the rear, chuntering nonstop about the absence of trollies. She attempted to keep up by juggling her abundance of bags. Her holdall swung by her knees, almost knocking her to the ground, but her determined facial expression stopped Miles from asking if she needed any help. He knew her answer would be in the negative.

At the entrance, the terminal doors slid open and thick, hot air smothered them in an instant. The heady mix of spices, fried food, exhaust fumes and body odour attacked their olfactory organs, leaving them almost gagging for pure oxygen. Hordes of people pushed shoved and shouted above the throng.

Oblivious to their plight, Amargeet forged ahead until he found what he was looking for. A large, black, shiny Chrysler with blacked-out windows sat at the curb, the engine running. He opened the boot and helped the trio deposit their luggage inside.

The trio was reluctant to leave their belongings until Amargeet slammed the boot shut and locked it. Pickpockets and opportunistic thieves lingered in their periphery waiting for their chance.

Liz entered the car determined to hold on to her holdall. Miles used the other door and Geoff followed him, forcing him to move along until his long legs were on either side of the centre reservation.

'Hello,' said nodding to the driver. She attempted a weak smile, but it looked more like a grimace.

The driver watched her enter from behind thick mirrored sunglasses but refrained from speaking.

Liz's eyebrow rose in a silent question to her two companions.

'So,' Geoff said, his voice jovial and excited. 'How far will we have to travel?'

The driver remained mute. His foot revved the engine, impatient to leave.

'Our destination is about a four-hour drive from here.' Amargeet answered.

The trio hesitated, waiting for him to extrapolate, but he fell silent. An uncomfortable pause stretched between them, wrapping itself around their necks, slowly strangling their vocal cords until they all felt at a loss for how to continue.

Amargeet sensed the inquietude and fiddled with the radio to find some music. A lyrical ghostly melody soon flooded the gaping silence as the driver zoomed away like he was in a Formula One race.

When they encountered heavy traffic, the driver slowed to a normal speed.

Geoff and Liz were soon dozing, their heads on Miles's shoulders despite the constant honking and shouting permeating the car from outside. He doubted he'd sleep, but his eyes grew heavy, and a yawn escaped from behind his lips. Just before his eyelids drooped, he thought he saw a thin wisp of white smoke slither from the CD cavity, but a second glance revealed nothing. He put it down to tiredness and soon fell asleep.

*

Liz nudged him awake. 'Miles, we're here. Wake up!'

He opened his eyes, squinting in the bright sunlight. The car had stopped in front of a dilapidated, two-story, ramshackle hotel in the centre of a small, rundown village. The hotel's light-pink paint crumbled to the dusty ground below it. Mangy dogs and barefoot kids in ragged clothes ran rampant on streets without sidewalks. A vendor stood on the corner, grasping the side of his small wooden fruit cart, bewildered by the appearance of the Europeans.

Geoff exited the air-conditioned car, looked up at the crumbling building, and crumpled up his nose. 'Is this it? Are we expected to stay here?'

Miles frowned. 'Keep your voice down. This is probably the best there is in such a small village. We'll have to make the most of it if we want to get into the heart of the sacred forest.'

Liz nodded. 'Yeah, Geoff, we're fortunate they have even allowed us to be here. There have been restrictions on forests since the 19th century.'

'Really?'

'Yeah. She's telling the truth,' Miles replied. 'Under British rule, local people lost their rights to use forest resources. Most of them were just foraging for food, but the British put a stop to it.'

'How do you know all this?' Geoff said.

Liz rolled her eyes. 'Research, Geoff, research. You should know what that is seeing as you're studying for a doctorate in botany.'

Geoff's eyes narrowed. 'Of course, I know what it is! I'm asking why you bothered to research antiquated laws from the eighteen hundreds.'

Liz resisted the urge to sigh. 'I don't enjoy going anywhere without finding out everything I can about the area first, and what I can expect there.'

Geoff shrugged. 'Fair enough. Don't get your knickers in a twist!'

Liz glared at him.

'It makes sense, I suppose,' he said, trying to appease her. 'Your research of the place, I mean. Shall we go into our not-so-five-star hotel, then?'

Miles and Liz nodded.

Amargeet stopped them when they headed to the boot of the car. 'Don't worry. I will have your belongings taken to your rooms.'

Liz tried to stare into his eyes through the mirrored sunglasses. It was impossible. She couldn't explain it, but both he and the driver unnerved her. An inner alarm bell clanged inside her head. She clutched her hand luggage bag to her chest. If she needed to flee, everything she would need was inside it.

A glance at Geoff and Miles confirmed they were not experiencing the same fear. They cajoled and jostled each other, laughing as they headed inside.

The dilapidated reception area of the hotel mirrored the hotel's façade. Faded, dated wallpaper peeling at the corners, threatened to plummet to the patchy light blue carpet under the trio's feet. A tired fan churned hot air around the reception desk and a weary young woman gave them a weak smile.

'Hello. You must be the three Botanists. Welcome. We have been expecting you.' She put her palms together and executed a slight bow.

Liz dug into her holdall and extracted her passport. The guys did the same.

The receptionist gave each a fleeting glance before handing them back. 'Thank you.' She handed over three keys.

'It looks like I'm on a different floor than you two,' Liz said, looking at the three keys. 'I'm not happy about that.'

The receptionist anticipated her demand for another room. 'Sorry, but the hotel is full right now. It is the festival of Diwali this weekend. It is the Indian festival of lights. It celebrates the victory of evil over good. Oh! I mean, good over evil.'

The trio didn't miss the receptionist's shudder.

'I may be able to find you another room next week.' She flashed her weak smile again.

Liz sighed; her level of disillusion sank even further. 'Where's the elevator?' her voice echoed her disappointment.

'There isn't one. You must use the stairs,' came the reply.

'Why does that not surprise me?' Liz's sarcasm was lost on the young woman but not her two travelling companions.

Miles rubbed her shoulder. 'Come on, Liz, it'll be fine.'

'Yeah. Right!' Liz muttered.

'That could be why Amargeet's offered to bring in the luggage,' Geoff said.

Miles eyed his small, frugally decorated room with disdain. A small double bed dressed in an orange fluffy eiderdown from the 1970s dominated the room. It reminded him of his grandmother's house. A flimsy single-door wardrobe flanked one side of the bed. A dilapidated bedside table with a wonky lamp sat at the other. Television didn't seem to have reached this far-flung location, and when he checked his phone, he had no internet signal either. A thin shelf ran along the wall opposite the bed, which housed an antiquated telephone, and a small mirror mottled with age spots stood beside it. He studied his reflection. Tiredness etched itself into his brow and highlighted in his eyes. His body cried out for sleep. He couldn't contain his disappointment. This part of India was hardly affluent, but he had expected more.

The botanist considered unpacking but decided against it. Perhaps they could find better lodgings later. As three scientists, here to study the indigenous plants and herbs for their doctorate degrees, he hadn't expected palatial accommodation, but he doubted they could stay in anything lower standard than their present digs.

Disgruntled, he left his room, pocketed his key, and strode along the corridor to Geoff's bedroom. The door was ajar. He leant in the entrance with his hands in the pockets of his jeans.

'Hi! Do you fancy a drink?'

'I sure do. Look at this dump. There isn't even a minibar!'

'Let's find Liz, then see if we can get some form of alcohol in this joint. If not, we can take a walk around the village. There must be somewhere that sells booze.'

'I could do with something to eat too. I'm starving. I could eat a scabby horse! Maybe there'll be a small supermarket in the village.'

Miles laughed. 'Huh! I doubt that. Maybe a corner shop if we're lucky.'

When Geoff closed his door, they sprang down the crumbling, wide stone steps to the floor below.

Liz jumped when they knocked on her door. She didn't like the place at all. Being one floor away from the men unnerved her even more. She felt more vulnerable and exposed.

When they told her their plan, she was itching to get outside.

They reached the reception area but, finding it unmanned, pocketed their keys and stepped outside into the overpowering heat. Like before, the mangy dogs and scraggily dressed children stopped chasing each other. Fascinated, they watch the trajectory of the three phytologists.

Geoff stopped in front of one small group. 'Where can we get a drink?' he mimed the action.

'Don't encourage them,' Liz replied. 'They'll never stop pestering us for money.'

Geoff ignored her. 'Alcohol,' he said, bending further towards them.

Miles rolled his eyes and shook his head. 'I'm sure that's not right. You can't ask kids where you can buy booze.'

'Hey. Listen. A drink is a drink. For them, my miming could mean coke or lemonade. And at this point, anything will do. Even a glass of cold water!'

'It's not advisable to drink the water here. Even bottled water can be tampered with,' Liz said.

Geoff rolled his eyes. 'Jesus, Liz. You should change your name to Siri!'

Liz scowled at him. Her lips pulled into a tight line. She didn't want to say anything she may regret, but he antagonised her to where she could rip his eyes out of their sockets. Liz imagined drawing a machete and slicing it across his neck in one swift movement to silence him. She would enjoy watching him crumple into a bloody heap at her feet.

'Look,' Miles said. Their eyes followed the trajectory of one little boy's skinny arm as he pointed to a small building down the street.

'Great. Thank you,' Geoff said. He shook his hand and, just to further rile Liz, he pushed a rupee into the child's hand.

Before they could take two steps in the right direction, every child in the vicinity followed behind them.

Liz groaned. 'I told you! Now we'll never get rid of them. From what I researched, all Indian kids follow foreigners hoping to get some money, sweets or other little presents.'

'I've heard that too,' Miles replied. 'It's as if they have built-in radars to track strangers.'

Liz wafted her hands at the group of kids. 'Shoo! Go away!'

'Liz! Don't be so rude. They're just curious,' Geoff said. 'They're only kids. I bet it's the first time they've seen a foreigner.'

'Maybe, but I find it annoying.'

*You find everything annoying!* Geoff thought. He hoped Liz would chill out soon because the thought of spending the next three months with her was depressing him already. She was so judgemental and thought she knew everything. Couldn't she just relax and enjoy the moment?

'I think this must be the bar,' Miles said, his words slicing through the increasing animosity.

The tiny establishment had such a small doorway, the two guys had to bend forward to enter. Inside, the room held a tiny bar running along the back wall, four mismatched tables and an assortment of odd chairs. In one corner, an antiquated jukebox displayed a selection of 1960s Western music; the tones of the Beatles singing "Lucy in the Sky with Diamonds" welcomed them inside.

'Namaste,' said the elderly man behind the bar.

The trio wondered if they had woken him up. His eyes swam with liquid, and he squinted at them as though his vision hadn't quite focused yet. He was bent almost double and grasped the bar for support.

'Namaste. Do you speak English?' Miles' voice rose, assuming the old man's hearing had also deteriorated along with his sight.

'Yes,' the man replied. 'I suppose you travellers are looking to drown your sorrows in alcohol, no?' He didn't wait for a reply. Three small bottles of Indian beer appeared on the cracked bar top. He struggled to remove the tops before pushing them towards the trio.

'Thank you,' Miles said, taking a seat on a wobbly bar stool. The others followed suit.

'It's true, we have just arrived, but we're not travellers,' he said, wondering if his choice of words was too complicated for the elderly man. 'We are botanists. We've come to study the indigenous plants and herbs in the forest here.'

He wasn't expecting the reaction he received. The barista stepped backwards, grabbed his heart, and almost collapsed into a chair.

'Oh, my God! Are you okay?' Liz asked. She wondered what the legal implications would be if the old guy dropped dead in front of them. But it didn't stop her from heading behind the bar to help him.

The man grappled inside his shirt pocket, pulled out a pill between his crooked, leatherlike fingers and slipped it under his tongue.

Liz loosened his shirt collar. She snatched up a yellowed magazine and fanned him.

'I'll get you some water,' Miles said, running behind the bar. He found a glass and scanned the area for a tap. When he turned it on, thick brown sludge oozed out of it like lightly diluted excrement. The smell wasn't much better. Miles retched and turned it off.

'Here!' Liz reached inside a fridge and pushed a small bottle of water into his hands. 'Give him that.' She wanted to help, but was now reticent to approach the old man. She didn't know why.

Miles handed him the opened bottle, and they watched him take a few sips. Flecks of colour returned to his face, but his eyes remained bulbous and full of fear.

'Don't go into the forest.'

Geoff stifled a laugh. When the others didn't join him, he took a swig of warm beer, but he couldn't remain silent. 'Why ever not?'

'Many men have entered, but few have returned.'

'Why? What's in there? Tigers?'

The old man's body quivered with fear. His eyes bulged in their sockets and flicked left and right. His spindly finger pointed at all three of them. 'I can tell you no more. Just stay away.'

'O...kay,' Geoff's prolonged sarcastic reply accentuated his disbelief. While making the other two squirm with discomfort.

The man's eyes narrowed. 'Beware of false promises, for they will be your downfall and remember; eyes are the windows to the soul.' He slumped even further into his chair. His eyes closed.

'Is he dead?' Liz said. Fear laced her words. She looked at Miles to provide the answer.

He felt the Indian's pulse. 'No. I think he'll be fine.'

Liz shivered, and not from the cold. She couldn't decide which place was the creepiest, the bar or the hotel. She wished she'd never come. Miles had been the one who had invited her to accompany him. She had planned to follow a different route for her doctorate, but the thought of travelling alone with him had pulled her in that direction. They had always been great friends, but for a long time, she had yearned for a more intimate relationship.

When she discovered Miles had also invited Geoff, it was too late for her to back out. She had imagined full days by Miles' side, working and studying together like they'd done since high school. They had spent summers practically living in each other's houses. She had even learnt sign language so she could interact with James, Miles's younger, non-verbal brother. But during all those years, Miles had never approached her romantically. The timing always seemed to be off. When he was dating someone, she wasn't and vice versa. She had truly believed this would be their chance, but Geoff had hindered that idea and she hated him for it.

She believed there had always been a spark between Miles and her, a tiny ember burning in the background, just waiting for a chance to burst into flame. But as she studied the two guys checking on the Indian, niggling doubts told her she may have read Mile's signals completely wrong. Maybe he'd invited her there purely for study. Since they had set off, nothing even slightly romantic had occurred. He hadn't even offered to help with her copious amount of luggage at the airport.

Her hopes of an amorous encounter slowly began to die. He saw her as his best friend, but nothing more. Even as she tried to convince herself their romantic connection was not about to happen, deep inside her bruised heart, a tiny ember of hope still shone in the darkness.

'I think this might be a good time to head back,' Miles said. 'Let's leave him to sleep.' He pushed some coins onto the bar. 'We've got a long day ahead of us tomorrow, and I think we could all do with a good night's sleep.'

Liz nodded, but didn't want to go back to her room alone. She doubted she'd sleep at all. The eerie, cold bedroom with its flimsy wooden door gave her the creeps. One hefty kick was all it would take for an intruder to gain entry.

A wicked thought flashed through her mind. Maybe this was her chance. She could tap on Miles's room and tell him she was afraid. He wouldn't turn away a damsel in distress. Or would he? The thought of him inviting her into his bed made her body tingle with excitement.

But then visions of her mother's words swam through her befuddled brain.

*'If he hasn't made a move after all these years, you're either not his type, or he's not into girls.'*

'MUM!' Liz had exclaimed, but now her mother's words of wisdom rattled the cage of her brain, casting doubt over everything. His amorous encounters as a teen hadn't lasted long, but that didn't mean he could be gay, did it?

The trio wandered outside. On the short walk back, Liz glanced in Miles' direction, hoping for some verification of his feelings.

Miles felt her gaze. He smiled, then looked away.

Liz's fears augmented. There was only one way to put herself out of this misery and that was to go to his room and seduce him. She fell silent as they ambled back. Her mind worked overtime while she planned how to do it.

A thin mist hung over the town and appeared to be creeping towards the dusty streets. Miles shivered. The murky haze reminded him of the odd sliver of thin white smoke he thought he'd seen coming from the CD player. A frown creased his brow. He hated when he couldn't scientifically deduce a quandary. He cast his eyes to what was left of the cold dark grey slated sky.

'The weather doesn't look good,' he said. 'I've heard bad weather plagues this part of India; primarily heavy rains and thick fog. I hope our first excursion to the forest tomorrow won't be cancelled.'

'Me too,' Liz gave him one of her captivating smiles. 'Although, after what the old barman said I can't help but feel a little preoccupied.'

'Ah! Don't listen to him,' Geoff replied. 'That's just a load of old poppycock. Wives' tales and Indian superstitions. You're a scientist. You shouldn't believe in all that mumbo jumbo.'

Liz glared at him. 'I know that. I said it unnerved me, that's all.'

Miles grasped her wrist and squeezed. Liz wasn't sure if it was to show he was on her side or to quieten her down. Either way, she basked in the tiny crumb of attention he had thrown her way.

Back at the hotel, the trio split up, said goodnight, and headed to their rooms.

After a long shower in tepid water, Liz shivered in her thin nightdress on the top of the bed. Her mind raced with ideas, and her body yearned for his touch. Her front teeth gnawed on her bottom lip. Should she do it? Dare she go to Miles' room? What if he rejected her advances? Or, worse still, what if she disappointed him?

She climbed off the bed and paced the small room. How long should she wait?

Outside her window, torrential rain had converted into hailstones. They pelted the window frames, hitting the glass like tiny bullets, and somehow urged her on. The battering sound converted into a single word that hypnotised her brain. Go, go, go!

Empowered, Liz slid off the bed, grabbed her dressing gown, and pushed her feet into her slippers. It was now or never.

Miles stared out of the window into the blackened night. He wanted to sleep but couldn't. He had dreamed of coming to India to research native plants, but the barman's warning, plus the terrible weather, made him worry he'd made a huge mistake.

A hesitant knock on the door pulled him away from the window. It was so faint he paused, wondering if he'd imagined it.

There it was again.

He crossed the room and stood at the door reticent to open it. 'Who is it?'

'... It's me, Liz. Can I come in?'

Bewildered, Miles opened the door. 'Liz? Are you okay? What's wrong?'

Her eyes threatened to brim over with unshed tears. 'Can I stay here tonight? I can't settle down there. I just don't feel safe.'

Miles opened the door wider. 'Of course. Come in.' He placed a hand on her shoulder, helping her inside.

Liz encircled his torso with both arms, her head leaning on his chest, listening to his beating heart. If there was a heaven, then this was what it must feel like.

They stood in silence. Liz breathed in his manliness, relishing every second, determined to remember the moment forever. Miles, perturbed by her fragility, held her close, hoping to soothe her confusion and pain.

With his hands on both her shoulders, he held her at arm's length to stare into her eyes. 'What's wrong, Liz?'

She mistook his actions as him pushing her away, distancing her. It weakened her resolve, but she was there, in his room. It was now or never.

'I'm scared, Miles. It's this place. I don't feel safe. There's something sinister here. I feel it. Something dark and overpowering.'

Miles fought the urge to belittle her words. 'Liz, I admit the hotel is far from what I imagined, but it's just old and rundown. We are in the middle of a tiny backward village in India. These people have nothing. But that doesn't mean there's anything bad here.'

'What about the old man in the bar? What about his warning?'

Miles couldn't admit the barista's words had unnerved him, too. 'These people are superstitious. They believe in the myths and legends passed down through the generations. You should take it all with a pinch of salt.'

Liz wasn't so sure. It seemed bizarre he would downplay the locals' suspicions and tell her to dismiss them by quoting a European one.

She frowned. 'But he seemed so sincere. And what about the receptionist the way she shivered when she confused good and evil? That was weird too.'

'Come on,' he walked her towards the bed. 'Lie down. Everything will feel much better in the morning when you've had a few hours of sleep.'

Sleep was the last thing on Liz's mind. The almost primal urge to seduce Miles flooded her brain and refused to quieten. An inner sensor told her this could be her last chance to confess her true feelings to the man she had loved for years.

The double bed dominated the room and her thoughts.

Once they were under the covers, she would have to make her move. Her mouth lost all its spittle. Nerves jangled, sending her courage shivering into the darkness of her building doubt.

Miles got into bed. He pulled back the covers and patted the mattress, inviting her to join him. She tentatively slid under the sheets, well aware of his closeness. The heat from his body radiated toward her. On impulse, she snuggled into him, throwing one arm around his waist and hugging him tight. Miles reciprocated. He pulled her closer and kissed the top of her head.

Emboldened, Liz lifted her face towards his and kissed him on the lips. Her body flooded with dopamine, and her inner core throbbed in anticipation.

Miles was surprised, but when he returned the kiss with fervour, Liz had never felt so ecstatic. Their passion grew and Liz gave herself to him. They explored each other's bodies until dawn when the weather had quietened, and an uneasy silence fell upon the village.

*

Mile's mobile alarm woke them both. Liz squirmed with pleasure, remembering the previous night. Sleeping with Miles had been even better than she had imagined. He was an experienced and innovative lover who had fulfilled her every desire.

He smiled at her. A grin packed with illicit meaning.

'Good morning, beautiful.'

'Hi,' her voice sounded demure yet croaky.

'I hope you feel better this morning.'

A demure smile radiated from her face. 'Much better, thank you.'

'Great! Come on, let's go explore the,' he held up his fingers in inverted commas, 'enchanted forest with lions and tigers and bears. Oh, my!'

His attempt at comedy backfired. It left her shivering inside, but she pasted on a smile and tapped him playfully on the arm. 'Stop it!'

'Well, last night was unexpected. A great surprise, but not at all what I had envisaged.'

Liz cringed. Was he regretting it? 'I suppose I'd better go,' she said.

'Okay. I'll see you downstairs for breakfast.'

Liz nodded, unsure she trusted her voice. She grabbed her dressing gown, stuffed her feet into her discarded slippers, and headed for the door. As she opened it, Miles pulled her back. He kissed her so deeply, her lips felt bruised.

His eyes swam with emotion tinged with sexual prowess. 'Yeah, see you down there.'

Liz scuttled down the corridor and skipped down the stone steps, hoping to reach her room without being seen.

The trio met in the dining room where a frugal breakfast of toast and selected fruits seemed to be the only food available.

They ate in relative silence, but Geoff sensed the unspoken connection between his workmates and felt slightly isolated.

Amargeet sauntered into the dining room. 'Good morning,' he said. 'I trust you slept well?'

Although it evoked a reply, he didn't wait for one.

Geoff didn't miss the flash of a smile and the blush of a cheek between his two companions and was sure of his assumption. They had slept together the night before.

Amargeet realised he wasn't about to get a reply. 'I have a tuk-tuk waiting to take you to the forest.'

'Okay, let's do this!' Miles grinned with excitement.

Geoff sighed. 'Give us ten minutes to finish breakfast and get ready.'

Liz almost froze in her seat. Fear coursed through her veins like a train with failed brakes. She didn't want to go.

'Liz, are you alright?' Geoff had witnessed her fright.

'Yeah, yeah. I'm fine.'

'Right! Good. Let's meet in reception in ten minutes,' Miles said and strode from the table, leaving his almost untouched breakfast behind.

Liz felt abandoned. Miles' love of his career had outranked their night of lovemaking.

'Listen, Geoff,' she said. 'I know you think what the bartender said is superstitious nonsense, but promise me you'll be careful. Don't take any risks.'

Her sincerity surprised Geoff. He still believed the tales were mumbo jumbo, but he nodded with solemnity. 'I swear, I'll be careful.'

Liz exhaled. 'Great. I appreciate that, Geoff. See you in ten minutes.'

## Chapter Two

The battered tuk-tuk painted green and yellow, the colours of the Indian flag, stood with the engine idling at the kerb. Liz sniffed at the chosen transport. She would have preferred the huge black car from the day before.

'This looks like a death trap,' she muttered as the exhaust backfired and a cloud of black smoke billowed behind it.

'Will we all fit inside?' Geoff asked, his corpulent stomach protruding from the top of his colourful Bermuda shorts.

'We can try,' Miles replied.

The trio squashed into the back, while Amargeet climbed onto the back and hung on to the skeletal frame. He reminded Miles of an oversized spider, particularly with his mirrored sunglasses still covering his eyes.

The driver was a middle-aged man who coughed as he smoked a strong-smelling cigarette. He scratched the tough wrinkled skin on his tanned arms that resembled elephant hide as he glanced in the tiny rearview mirror, before pulling away from the kerb.

Liz pulled on Amargeet's shirt sleeve and into the annoying buzzing of the engine, she yelled: 'We found a little bar last night,

Amargeet. The owner told us we needed to be careful in the forest. He said many people enter, but few return. What does he mean?'

She watched his hands curled tighter around the metal frame of the tuk-tuk. He continued looking ahead.

'You shouldn't listen to him. He speaks rubbish.'

From his voice, Liz sensed his discomfort.

'But he seemed so sincere.'

Amargeet coughed. 'He is an old man. Maybe he is senile. Ignore him.'

'Even so...' she turned to Miles, or even Geoff for support.

They said nothing.

*I never said he was old,* she thought, as a frisson of fear sewed itself around her spine.

Geoff shivered in his seat. 'Burrh! Where has this mist come from? It was lovely and sunny when we set off. I'm going to freeze to death in the forest!'

'That's your own fault. Your attire is hardly appropriate for spending the day foraging for shrubs,' Liz replied. 'A beach in the Bahamas, maybe, but here! It's supposed to be one of the wettest places in India.'

'Oh, listen to the old Oracle here. Yesterday you had to show us how much you knew about the forest restrictions. Today's gonna be the weather. Well, bring it on!'

'It's basic common sense, Geoff. Instead of Bermuda shorts and a T-shirt, any normal person would have brought good stout walking boots, thick socks, and warm trousers. Kinda the things Miles and I are wearing!'

'Children, children, please. Stop bickering, we're almost there.' Miles said, trying to laugh off their animosity.

When the vehicle pulled off the road and travelled down a dirt path toward their destination, the fog thickened. It hung over the forest, darkening the undergrowth and dampening everything in sight.

At the main entrance stood a soldier. He wore camouflage gear, held a rifle, spoke into a walkie-talkie clipped to a lapel, and stood with his legs apart. He sported the same type of mirrored glasses Amargeet and yesterday's driver had worn.

Miles thought it odd, considering the weather. He also hated that he couldn't see the soldier's eyes and read what he was thinking.

Liz perused a thick iron fence that stood eight feet tall and was so long it disappeared into the rolling mist like some sort of vortex was swallowing it up. Once again, she experienced a sinking sensation, as if she were making the biggest mistake of her life.

Amargeet jumped from the back of the vehicle. He leaned in toward them.

'Stay here. I must clear your entry with the soldier first.'

Geoff laughed. 'Ha! Clear your entry? That's got sexual connotations to it, don't you think?'

'Yeh! I never thought of it like that!' Miles replied. 'It's your dirty mind!'

Geoff's eyes narrowed. He turned to Liz. 'Hey. Do you need your entry clearing, Liz?'

'No! I do not!' she snapped.

Miles climbed out of the vehicle, laughing to himself.

Geoff followed him.

Liz remained seated. She felt her fear rising notch by notch, but couldn't explain why she was so scared.

Her eyes fell on the soldier. Why would there be an armed guard to protect a forest? Even though she knew about the laws and forest acts, a military presence seemed way over the top.

The driver, who had remained mute during the drive, coughed then muttered in English, in a voice so low, Liz almost missed it.

'Lady, please. Be careful in there,' he whispered. 'Follow the soldier's instructions and don't stray from the paths. It's true; many people visit the forest, but few return.'

Liz's heartbeat quickened. 'Why? What happens to them?' Liz asked, gripping the seat in front of her.

Amargeet turned and strode toward them. Miles followed him.

The tuk-tuk driver picked up an aged newspaper and pretended to read. 'Nobody knows,' he whispered.

Liz bit her bottom lip, unsure whether to follow her instinct and run away; flee as far and as fast as she could from the forest or follow the man of her dreams into... who knew what?

Miles recognised her reluctance. He reached for her hand and squeezed.

'Come on. Don't worry. I'm sure we'll be fine. I doubt the Indian Government would permit us entry if there was something sinister inside.'

Liz nodded, but avoided eye contact as she left the vehicle. Her brain was screaming *Runaway! Hide! Get the hell out of India! Who would care if someone went missing in a forest in the middle of nowhere?*

The sound of the disappearing tuk-tuk sealed her fate. Amargeet had also vanished. She had no choice but to follow Miles and Geoff into the heavy foliage.

*

The winding path grew narrower the further they walked into the undergrowth. A thin sprinkling of gravel that had once crunched beneath their feet had given way to yellowed sand. It reminded Liz of the yellow brick road and all the strange occurrences that had happened in the weird land of Oz. Was this another sign that she should turn back and head for the entrance? She spun around, but the heavy mist seemed to have followed them. She couldn't see more than a few metres in front of her face. "There's no place like home," ran on a loop through her brain.

Abruptly, Miles dropped Liz's hand and strode ahead, his eyes alight, drinking in his surroundings. He couldn't believe they were finally traversing the forest floor in search of rare and maybe even unknown plants and herbs.

In front of him, the mist began to clear. Bright sunlight shone on the tallest trees, burning the natural overhead canvas with its heat. Below, weaker rays filtered to the forest floor and caressed the growing seedlings, encouraging them to turn toward the light.

Annoyed the forest seemed more important than her, Liz strode behind Miles, trying to keep up.

His excitement was palpable. 'Just look at this place! It's simply amazing!' he said, stopping with his hands on his hips like some sort of superhero to stare into the undergrowth.

'Look over there!' Geoff's finger shook in wonderment. 'Those tiny dancing lights. If I didn't know any better, I'd say that was fairy dust.'

Liz clicked her tongue. 'Yeah, right! If they grant you a wish, perhaps you can ask for some decent clothes.'

Geoff ignored her. Despite the sun, he was cold, but didn't want to admit it. 'No. I'd ask them to put you in a better mood!'

'Shut up, Geoff!'

'No, you shut up, Liz. You're really getting on my nerves!'

'Likewise!'

'Hey, guys! Look at that! Can it...? It can't be!' Miles pointed into the foliage at a tall, bright orange plant with heavy shiny leaves that seemed to glisten in the limited sunlight. He charged toward the middle of an overgrown patch. 'I can't believe it! It's a miracle!' He fell to his knees and stared at the specimen like a love-sick teen. 'I've found it already! This is the Tetintrey plant. It is thought to be extinct. The Indians believe it stops ageing. Its biological name means "Hour-Glass". The Shamans believe it can virtually stop time. If we study how the properties of this plant work, I believe we could stop the ageing process. This could make us millionaires.'

He lifted his head to the heavens and laughed out loud. His voice echoed through the trees and returned to him. 'I can't believe my luck! That's incredible!'

Miles turned around to witness their reaction, but they had disappeared. An overwhelming sense of fear charged up his spine. The words of the barista came back to haunt him, adding to his anguish.

'Liz? Geoff? Where are you? If this is a joke, it isn't funny!' He stood motionless, listening to the silence.

The dulcet tones of a paradise flycatcher bird broke the moment. Miles searched the trees to find the feathered singer. At his feet, he found a male peacock. It extended its feathers, showed off its magnificent plumage, and seemed to laugh at his predicament.

When his eyes fell to the track again, Miles saw Liz and Geoff standing there giggling.

'Got ya!' Geoff laughed.

Liz clung to his arm.

Miles didn't like it. 'Where did you go?' he frowned. 'That wasn't funny. I thought the barman's prediction had come true!' Liz walked toward him, then rubbed his arm and smiled up at him. When he looked into her eyes, she blinked, and his fear vanished. Her face radiated her love for him. He felt strangely sated, as though they had lain in the forest and repeated what they had started the night before.

Geoff tapped him on the back. 'It was a joke, Miles. Where else would we be? We've been here all the time.'

Liz giggled again.

Miles frowned, assuming it must be a private joke between the two of them. He didn't pursue it. For once, it pleased him they were finally getting along. He wondered if Geoff's wish for Liz to be in a better mood had actually come true.

'So, Miles, shall we help you get some samples?' Geoff said.

'Of course. We're all in this together.'

Liz grinned and winked at him. 'We sure are.'

The morning passed in a blur. There were so many species that they had never come across before and their samples were soon adding up.

'Why don't we stop for lunch?' Liz suggested. 'Amargeet told me there's a clearing around here somewhere and he has set up a picnic for us all.'

'Great!' Geoff said. 'I'm starving, I must admit.'

'When did he say that?'

'What?'

'How do you know there's a clearing and a picnic?'

Liz scowled.

Geoff patted his back. 'Just as we entered the forest. You were too interested in your surroundings to pay attention.'

Liz linked her arm through Miles'. 'Are you coming or what?'

It was Miles' turn to grin. 'Of course. I'm famished. Who would have thought that picking a few samples would make a guy so hungry?'

They trampled through the undergrowth until they came across the clearing. The sun, radiant above them, covered the ground like a warm eiderdown. Birds warned each other with chirps and whistles of the trio's arrival, while skittish rabbits peeked through the grass out of curiosity. A family of deer stopped grazing to look at the intruders before scampering into the undergrowth. Geoff threw himself onto the thick picnic blanket to bask in the sunshine. A hamper sat open, and a bottle of white wine lay tilted in a silver-coloured bucket full of ice, as though it too was enjoying the sunshine.

Liz knelt on the blanket and peered into the hamper. 'Wow! There's a veritable feast here.' She extracted roast beef sandwiches with horseradish sauce, and salad sandwiches, so laden with ingredients the contents threatened to fall. Thick chocolate cake tantalised their tastebuds, and fluffy scones with cream made them drool.

'These are all my favourite things! It's as if Amargeet read my mind!' Miles's smile almost reached his ears. He was so delighted by the unexpected contents.

'Mine too,' Liz replied.

'Ditto,' Geoff said.

They sat in silence, taking in the serenity of the forest scenery while munching on the fare.

Geoff opened the wine and poured it into three glasses. He held up his drink. 'Cheers! Let's hope every day will be like this one!'

Miles clinked his glass with Geoff's.

Liz did the same. 'Hear, hear!'

'It's incredible, don't you think?' Miles said. 'I mean, the sun is out. We've found so many of the plants we imagined spending months searching for, and now we have this lovely picnic in such a beautiful spot. It almost feels too good to be true.'

'You can say that again,' Geoff smiled. 'Who would have thought we could be so lucky?'

They clinked glasses a second time and fell into a companionable silence.

The food soon disappeared. The trio imbibed the wine and lay back on the blanket with their hands under their heads, basking in the sunlight.

*

The drive back in the tuk-tuk to the hotel was shorter than Miles remembered. And when he spied Amargeet standing outside the hotel with all their baggage, he was even more surprised.

'What's the meaning of this?' he snapped, annoyed to think the Indian had rummaged around in his personal belongings.

He turned to the others for moral support. They nodded in agreement.

'You have arrived earlier than we expected,' Amargeet explained. We have found a much better hotel for you to stay in. 'Please, follow me.' He pointed down the street where the black car stood, its engine idling. The trio ambled toward it and climbed inside.

'Where exactly is this new hotel?' Liz enquired, while Amargeet stored all their luggage inside the car.

'It's much closer to the forest,' Amargeet replied. 'From there, you can walk to your destination within five minutes.'

'That'll be handy, won't it?' Geoff said. 'I'd rather walk to the forest than squash myself in another tuk-tuk with you two!'

'HEY!' Miles laughed.

Liz shook her head, but a small smirk passed across her face.

Amargeet waited until they were all inside the car. He turned his head to the driver. 'If you please.'

'Hey, Miles, wake up. We're here.'

The botanist forced his eyes open. 'How long have I been asleep?'

'Not long,' Liz said. 'But look at this,' she pointed out of the window. 'How's that for an upgrade?'

When Miles saw the imposing hotel looming before them, he gasped. 'Wow! This is more like it!'

'It sure is,' Geoff replied.

'Go inside and register,' Amargeet replied. 'I'll get the porter to bring your luggage to your rooms.'

The trio didn't need telling twice.

This time, the receptionist gave the guys a room together and Liz's accommodation was just two doors down.

Within minutes, the trio was exploring the facilities. The hotel boasted three different cuisines: Indian, Far Eastern and European.

Miles grinned. 'This is excellent. There's something for everyone.'

The others nodded in assent.

They strolled through the hotel floor by floor, finding the indoor heated swimming pool and a huge outdoor pool. A gym, a massage parlour, a dining room, a coffee shop, a casino, a pub, and a theatre to name but a few of the almost endless facilities.

'Who would have thought there'd be such luxury in a tiny little place such as this?' Miles said.

'Who indeed?' Liz replied.

'I wonder why they didn't bring us here, to begin with?'

Liz shrugged and wrapped a hand around his arm. 'Who cares? We're here now.'

Geoff nodded. 'Alcohol! That's what we need. Come on. Let's find ourselves a watering hole.'

They hunkered down in the pub for a few drinks before bed. Then, just after midnight, they retired for the evening.

*

The next morning, feeling refreshed, Miles showered and donned his attire to visit the forest again. Geoff was already up. He had left a note to say he was having breakfast in the restaurant below.

Miles headed to Liz's quarters to see if she wished to join them. He suddenly felt slightly repentant and stupid. He hadn't thought to go to Liz's room the previous night, but his brain felt foggy and disorientated. He didn't even remember getting to bed. He blamed the alcohol mixed with the euphoria of finding all the plants the day before.

He knocked and waited, trying to decide what to say when she opened the door. He would need to make things right. When he received no reply, he knocked again. His ear pressed to the door. He listened for movement. The room was as quiet as a grave. When he tried the handle, it surprised him to find it unlocked.

'Liz?' he called into the silence. 'Liz, are you here? I'm coming in.'

The emptiness enveloped him as he stepped inside. The room was devoid of any personal possessions. Liz was nowhere to be seen.

Confused, Miles stood in the middle of the room, unable to fathom what had happened. 'Liz?' He recognised the distress in his voice. It echoed around the empty room, giving him a foreboding feeling that he couldn't quite tame.

He sped to the dining room where Geoff was tucking into a hearty breakfast.

'Morning, Miles, can you believe it? They even have full English breakfasts. Just look at this!'

Miles glanced at the humongous plate of food, but his mind was elsewhere. 'I've just been to Liz's room. Her things aren't there. Do you know what's going on?'

Geoff reached into his pocket. 'I found this under the door this morning. It's addressed to you.' He handed over a small light blue envelope.

Miles stared at it. He wondered why Geoff would take it if the letter wasn't for him.

'Open it,' Geoff said through a mouthful of food.

Miles tore into the envelope and read the letter.

Miles, please, forgive me, but I think I made a horrible mistake coming here. I have decided to leave. You and Geoff should do the research together. I will write my doctorate on a different subject. Under the circumstances, I think it's better this way. I'm sorry for wasting your time.

Love, Liz. xx

There were two kisses which, considering their intimate evening two nights ago, seemed rather lacking. His eyes swung to Geoff.

'She's gone.'

'What do you mean?'

'She's left. She doesn't want to be part of our team anymore.'

'Ridiculous!' Geoff grabbed the letter and read it for himself. 'How weird!' He wiped a splodge of grease from his chin with a cotton napkin.

'I don't understand it,' Miles said. 'Last night, I thought all three of us were getting on great.' He sank into the nearest chair, staring at the note as if the words would change if he read and re-read it.

'Well, don't worry about me running out on you. I'm here to stay,' Geoff said. 'Come on. Eat something, Miles. We've got a busy day ahead of us. You will need your strength.' He pushed a plate of food towards him, then stabbed a sausage on his own plate and chomped on it as if he hadn't eaten in a long time.

*

After breakfast, they met Amargeet at the reception desk. He stood with his hands clasped before him and bowed his head when they approached.

'Good morning. I regret to inform you this will probably be the last time you will see me.'

'That's a shame,' Geoff said, his voice devoid of any genuine emotion.

'My last assignment is to show you the way to the forest.'

'We may need your help,' Miles said, staring into the Indian's mirrored glasses. 'Liz has left. Could you help us find her?'

Amargeet shrugged. He appeared non-plussed. His top lip curled upwards into a snarl. 'Few people can accept life in India. Many foreigners return much quicker than they expected.'

Miles found his response rather cold and lacking sentiment. He stared at the Indian, lost for words. He guessed he'd have to investigate himself.

They strode in silence toward the forest and, as Amargeet had said, they arrived in less than five minutes. The same soldier with the mirrored shades stood guard and moved aside to let them pass.

Miles felt strangely privileged to be allowed entry. He nodded to the guard and gave him a slight smile that wasn't reciprocated.

'What do you want to do today, Miles?' Geoff asked as they strolled along the thin gravel path.

'The same as yesterday. Look for more specimens.'

'Fine. Anything in particular?'

'No. I'd like more specimens like the ones we've already found. Maybe older examples, so we can test the validity and strength of each one. But this is your investigation as much as mine. If you want to do something else, just tell me.'

'No. Whatever you want to do is fine with me,' Geoff replied. 'I'll follow your lead.'

Both men wandered around the forest, but Mile's heart wasn't in it. He couldn't stop thinking about Liz's desertion. Of his two companions, he would have wagered good money Geoff would be more likely to leave.

Liz had been a constant companion since they started high school. They did everything together. She had raved about the trip before they left. She talked about nothing else. Why would she leave him now? It made little sense. It annoyed him she had slunk away in the middle of the night, like a criminal on the run rather than face him and tell him why she wanted to leave. It wasn't like her. She had always been confrontational. e equated her to a little Yorkshire Terrier.

'Hey, Miles, come on, cheer up. You're living an experience of a lifetime. We are in a protected forest, searching for things we never thought we'd get the chance to see.'

'I know. You're right, Geoff. It's just, I can't get over Liz leaving like that. It's so unlike her. Why wouldn't she talk to me about it first? I just don't get it.'

'Because she's a woman!' Geoff said, trying to make light of the situation. 'You and I both know they are strange unfathomable creatures. She'll come round to our way of thinking. Just leave her to get whatever it is out of her system.'

Miles nodded, but he wasn't convinced. 'Okay. I suppose you're right.'

At noon, Geoff wandered over to Miles. 'Hey, shall we go to the clearing and eat? I'm famished!'

Miles nodded. He, too, was hungry, yet still preoccupied by Liz's disappearance.

The two men strolled in companionable silence towards the clearing. Geoff leading the way.

'Can you hear that?' Mile asked.

'Hear what?'

'That singing. It's faint as if it's far away, but it's the most beautiful melody. Can't you hear it?'

Geoff shrugged. 'No. I can't hear anything.'

Miles shrugged. He continued walking, but the music seemed to seep through his skin. It entered his darkest recesses and filled him with a sensation of inner peace, tranquillity, and contentment.

When they arrived at the clearing, their mouths dropped open. Two young women, barely out of their teens were sitting on the picnic blanket eating what appeared to be the guys' lunch.

'Hey!' Geoff shouted, perturbed that his food was being consumed by two unknown women. 'What do you think you're doing?'

When both girls looked in their direction, Miles, lost for words, gawped at their beauty. He had never seen such stunning women in his life. Both had long hair flowing down their backs, to their hourglass waists. One was blonde the other brunette. Both had the most amazing green eyes that sparkled in the sunlight. Their tight-fitting tops and figure-hugging trousers showed they had curves in all the right places. Their skin was almost opaque. He wondered how long they had been in the forest and why they wouldn't seek the sunshine to colour their skin.

'I beg your pardon?' said the brunette, focusing on Geoff and pulling Miles back to the present.

'I said, you're eating our lunch!' Geoff replied.

'Huh! I beg to differ. Amargeet told us there would be a picnic basket in the clearing and we should help ourselves!'

Miles grabbed Geoff's wrist before he said anything more detrimental.

'She could be telling the truth,' he whispered. 'Amargeet said at breakfast that it was the last time we would see him. This lunch probably isn't for us at all.'

Geoff's puffed-out chest deflated. 'Then, I wish he'd told us! I would have brought some food from breakfast!'

The girls' laughter irked Miles more than he cared to admit.

Seeing his disillusioned expression, the blonde beckoned him toward them.

'Come. I think there has been a misunderstanding. Please, join us. There's more than enough food here for four people.' She patted the blanket, inviting them to sit.

Geoff glanced at Miles. 'What do you think we should do?'

'I think, considering we are hungry, it would be rude not to accept.' He dropped to his knees and held out his hand.

'Hi, I'm Miles and this is Geoff. We are botanists, out here investigating and collecting data for our doctoral thesis.'

'I'm Bella and this is Phoebe,' said the blonde. 'We are also botanists.'

'But you can call me Fée,' Phoebe interrupted with a lyrical French accent. She shook Geoff's hand and cast him a coquettish smile as he sat down beside her.

'What made you choose this place?' she asked.

'Miles found it. He was on the internet researching indigenous plants from around the world. We are searching for specimens with qualities linked to youthfulness and flawless skin. Or at least that's our primary aim.'

'Ah! So, you call yourselves botanists, but in reality, you are adventurers searching for the elixir of youth,' Bella jested. She jabbed Miles in the chest and ran her nail almost down to his waist. The unfamiliar touch sent frissons of pleasure radiating through his body.

Her eyes narrowed. 'What would you say if we said we had found something better?'

'Like what?' He couldn't seem to concentrate.

Her eyes sparkled. 'We have discovered the secret to eternal life!'

The once pleasurable sensation grabbed hold of Miles's gut and squeezed it in a vice-like grip. Confused, he grabbed his stomach and stared into her green eyes.

'I'm sorry. What?'

'Yeah. Fée and I are both over two thousand years old.'

Miles stared at her, lost for words. Flabbergasted, he felt his blood pressure rise until he thought he would experience a heart attack. They couldn't have found that. It would be so unfair. His idea of developing a cream to maintain youth seemed trivial compared to Bella's statement. This was to be his life's work!

'No! you can't have.' His words sounded like a whisper whipped away by the breeze.

Geoff broke the spell. 'Ha, ha! hilarious ladies, you had us going for a second there!'

The girls giggled, breaking the tension.

The grip on Miles's stomach lessened, his heart rate reduced, and he faked a laugh along with the others. Relief filled his insides. He still had a goal. He could continue his search.

'How clever of you to find this place, Geoff,' Fée said, changing the subject. 'We didn't know we weren't the only ones here.'

Geoff looked momentarily embarrassed, then raised his wine glass. 'Yeah, well, cheers ladies. Here's to many happy days working together.'

Miles frowned. Why would Geoff say that? Why would he want Bella and Fée to accompany them? What would stop the girls from stealing their idea and using it as their own? His eyes hardened. He glared at Geoff, but his so-called friend only had eyes for Fée.

'Cheers!' the girls clinked glasses and exchanged sly smiles with each other.

Geoff joined them in celebration.

Miles felt isolated. The three seemed comfortable in each other's company. He didn't want to share his findings or his work with anyone else but Geoff. Having two young interlopers he hardly knew could ruin everything. They may insist on being named in his work. They were too immature, and their youthful approach could hinder everything. How he wished Liz was still there.

'Come on, let's eat,' Fee said.

Geoff sat as close to Fee as he could.

Bella patted the blanket next to her. 'Come, Miles. Sit here.'

A reluctant sigh escaped his lips as he edged closer to her not to seem rude.

Just like the previous day, the hamper was full of delicious food, all of which Miles loved. The quartet chatted and ate in the amiable environment. Geoff and Fee were soon deep in conversation. Bella's tone and the wine soon made Miles doze off in the sun's warmth.

Miles shivered in the shade.

'Come on, sleepy head, it's time to go back to the hotel,' Geoff said.

'What? What time is it? I only closed my eyes for a second.'

'Hah! A second, he says. You've slept the entire afternoon. The girls and I have been collecting specimens all afternoon.'

'Why didn't you wake me?'

'I figured you could do with your sleep. I guess you've still got jet lag. It was a long flight over here.'

Miles nodded unconvinced. He sat up, rubbed his eyes then gasped.

'What is it?' Geoff saw his confused expression.

'I could have sworn I saw... No, never mind.' He shook his head. 'I guess I'm still half asleep.'

'But what was it?'

'You'll probably think I'm nuts, but I swear I saw Liz. Just for a second. She was staring at me. You don't think she's still here, do you?'

'Nah! Why would she say she was leaving and then hang around? No, mate. She's already on a flight back to the UK. Forget about her.'

'Maybe she decided to go it alone. She might have found something yesterday she thinks would be better than our idea and has branched out.'

His mind returned to their passionate night together in the grotty hotel. He couldn't imagine her abandoning him after that. But what if... A sick feeling invaded his stomach. What if his performance in bed had disappointed her? He was hardly a seasoned pro in the world of womanising. Maybe that was the reason she had gone. She didn't want a repeat performance. She had left the hotel during the night. Was that so she wouldn't have to face him or because she was upset he hadn't gone to her room last night?

Geoff's comment made the most sense. She was probably flying home right now. But he swore he'd seen her in the foliage. They had made eye contact. Why wouldn't she approach him and tell him what she had decided to do? Her facial expression was one of love and pity all rolled into one.

He mused over the words in her letter. She had said she was leaving the research for him and Geoff to do together and that she would choose a different subject. There was no mention of her leaving India. Perhaps she was still here. The thought intrigued him. He would love to know what she had discovered and what had changed her mind. Annoyance made his hands convert into fists. If she was still there, she should have the decency to tell him to his face!

His eyes searched the undergrowth for another glimpse of her. He blinked and saw Liz's face again, peering out from inside a bush. She mouthed something, but she was too far away for him to catch it. Her facial expressions showed anxiousness; the deep frown across her forehead, her darting eyes looking for danger and the stubborn streak he had grown up with was prominent on her face.

Suddenly, her head spun to the side. Fear overtook her frown, and she disappeared into the undergrowth.

A weird rolling white mist spread through the trees in seconds, like spilt wine soaking into a tablecloth, obliterating her image in a heartbeat.

He felt an arm link through his.

'Come on,' Bella said. 'Let's get back to the hotel.'

Miles glanced one last time into the fog-heavy foliage, then turned and walked away.

## Chapter Three

Time passed fleetingly. Before Miles knew it, a year had gone. His research had left him reeling with excitement. His foraging sessions in the forest with Geoff had resulted in them finding the ingredients to create a successful potion for permanent youthfulness. They spent their days in the forest searching for more specimens, growing their own, or in the laboratory producing the magic potion. Their nights they spent with Bella and Fée who had also joined his team.

Rather than spend all their free time together, both guys tended to be alone with their girls. Miles felt that hanging out every working day with Geoff was enough. They didn't need to live in each other's pockets. Both were grown men. What they did at night was their own affair.

Bella was pushing Miles into making a more permanent commitment. She wanted stability, something more than just cohabitation. He knew he was fortunate to have her. She was every man's dream. Every morning, she woke him with a breakfast tray full of all the things he loved. Cereals, toast, bacon and eggs, orange juice and a vitamin tablet. When he finished eating, she climbed back under the covers for their daily good morning coupling. He had never seen her angry, lose her temper, or become frustrated. She was the perfect woman, and she wanted him to make a commitment.

Miles understood, but something was holding him back.

That "something" was Liz.

Occasionally, when he was in the forest, he was convinced he saw flashes of her in the undergrowth, but whenever he headed in that direction, the strange, cold mist appeared. It enveloped her, wrapping itself around her like a heavy cloak until she disappeared before his eyes. He could never quite reach her.

On more than one occasion, he had pelted into the overgrown brush in search of her. But, like some weird magician wielding a magic wand, she had always vanished before he could reach her.

The last time had unnerved him even more. He knew it was her, yet she appeared older, as though the stress of being apart had aged her by ten years or more. For a few seconds, their eyes had made contact, and he registered the sorrow behind her welling tears. Her hands rose to her chest. 'You are in danger,' she said in sign language.

Miles had barely recognised her message before something disturbed her. Her head flicked to the right, and an expression of pure terror overwhelmed her face. She set off running into the thick foliage. Miles ran after her, but, like all the times before, she disappeared inside the thick grey mist before he could reach her. It made little sense!

He worried about her sanity. Was she living out in the dense forest alienated from society? If so, why? A woman alone would be easy pickings for any wild beasts or criminals that may wander onto her path.

Maybe Liz was slowly losing her mind. But she knew who he was, so why wouldn't she approach him? It was so confusing. He couldn't explain it, but he was certain she was still out there. Somewhere.

Miles had stopped telling the others about Liz's visitations. They never believed him and professed never to have seen her.

Bella's brow would deepen into a worried frown. Her teeth bit into her bottom lip and her eyes portrayed her worry. She thought he was losing his mind. She had told him to his face and had insisted he went to see a doctor, but Miles refused to consider it.

Sometimes, he wished he'd never confided in her. She was like a dog with a bone. She refused to let the matter drop. He wondered if it was jealousy that made her so antisocial.

Miles knew there was nothing wrong with his brain, although he couldn't explain the appearances of Liz when he least expected it. And now her advanced aging only added more thought to the puzzling mystery. It seemed odd he was working on the elixir of youth, yet Liz was ageing quicker than was humanly possible.

Geoff also dismissed Miles' "visitations" as wishful thinking. The botanist had confided in him about his passionate night together with Liz before she disappeared. Geoff tried to convince him that his hallucinations were due to his turbulent feelings of unrest. Liz had disappeared without saying goodbye, and Miles had no closure. But Miles couldn't escape the niggling feeling there was more to it than that. Why would she still be wandering around the forest, waiting to talk to him?

Bella's beautiful, soulful eyes would narrow whenever he mentioned Liz.

'Am I not enough? Would you prefer to be with her rather than me?' she said, sulking on their capacious double bed, her lithe body still wet with sweat after their torrid lovemaking.

Panicked, Miles rushed to her side. 'Of course, you are enough! You are all I'll ever need, but Liz is my friend. If she's still here and in trouble, I can't just ignore her. I need to help her.'

'Why would she still be here after all this time, Miles? We are living in a tiny village. You or Geoff would have seen her around here at some point. She can't still be in the forest. That's crazy!' Bella's bottom lip protruded in a sulk. Her arms folded across her pert breasts; the nipples tweaked to perfection.

Miles's eyes perused her body until he came to a mound of hair he knew so well.

Bella watched his facial expression and ran her hand down her flat stomach, past the mound between her legs and down her thigh.

'Come here,' she said, licking her lips and opening her legs to allow him a glance at what was to come.

Miles groaned, his bulging erection pulsating inside his jeans, fighting to be free. He ripped off the garments and crawled up the bed like a rabid dog going in for the kill.

Bella squirmed beneath him, a sly smile on her face. 'Come here, you beast,' her sultry voice made it impossible to ignore her.

Miles obeyed.

All thoughts of Liz evaporated from his mind.

The days passed in a haze of brilliant sunshine, and the nights they spent clasped together in an amorous embrace. Mile became so infatuated with Bella that he could think of nothing else. Her beauty overshadowed everyone else in the village.

Being with her overshadowed everything else. He still worked in the laboratory and visited the forest, but now, his academic dreams seemed less important, and he wandered around in a dream.

He met several biologists and other professionals who had come to this small part of India for various reasons. Some came to make seismic studies of the land, while others explored the unusual weather conditions. Some believed aliens roamed the forest. Others discovered the village by accident while hiking. They passed the time of day with each other, but their main reason for remaining in the tiny village was the partners they had met, who never left their sides.

Another year passed. Bella and Miles were married. It was a small ceremony in a tiny, pristine chapel on the edge of the village which Miles couldn't remember ever seeing before.

Geoff was the best man, and Fée was the matron of honour. Bella's younger sisters were the bride's maids.

Her parents had caused quite an impact when they appeared in the village. The villagers fell silent as though royalty had arrived. They all smiled and nodded, enthralled and delighted that Bella's parents had spoken to them. Some bowed their heads in reverence, but Miles, infatuated with Bella, only wanted her happiness and he didn't notice.

His wife-to-be introduced him to her parents before they wandered around shaking hands and chatting to everyone. It didn't occur to Miles how odd it was to meet his prospective parents-in-law for the first time on his wedding day.

The opulence of the affair overwhelmed him.

The wedding gifts the bride and groom received were not at all what he had expected. Thick gold chains, precious stones, an abundance of food, and live animals such as goats, chickens and other fowl that strutted around the village as if they owned it. Flabbergasted by the unusual gifts, Miles wondered where they were supposed to keep the livestock, considering they still lived in the hotel.

'We have bought you a small parcel of land in the forest, son. You can keep the livestock there.' Siod, Bella's father said, as if he'd read his son-in-law's mind.

'That's extremely generous of you, sir.' His brow furrowed. 'But, is that even allowed? I thought the forest was heavily protected, specifically for that reason.'

Siod waved him away. 'Don't you worry about that. I pulled a few strings, that's all. You are one of us now, my son, and always will be.' He patted Miles on the shoulder, then strode away.

A niggling doubt flashed through Miles' brain. Images of Liz telling them on their first day there, that it was a privilege to enter the forest at all. How could he now own a piece of it? Was that even allowed? His eyes searched the forest in the distance, looking for answers.

Bella appeared by his side. She squeezed his hand and once he glanced into her vivid green eyes, his turbulent thoughts dissipated from his mind.

'Come. The banquet is ready.' She took his hand and led him back to the group.

One long table covered in white muslin hosted an array of food. Various cuts of succulent meat, an amalgam of vegetables, fruit, rice, and potatoes covered the top. Yellow buttered sweetcorn made his mouth water, and a selection of cakes stood on a side table. A small quartet sat to one side playing a haunting melody that seemed to enter Miles' very soul and fill him with ecstatic euphoria that he couldn't explain.

After eating, everyone drank wine and danced into the night.

Bella was constantly by his side. A squeeze of his hand, a fluttering of her eyelashes and a coquettish smile constantly reassured him he had made the right decision.

## Chapter Four

The next morning, like every other day, Miles and Geoff walked in companionable silence toward the forest. They set about collecting samples, both wandering off in different directions in search of more.

As Miles foraged, he noticed a gentle clicking sound. It intrigued him. Since his arrival in India, he had spent so many hours in the forest that he thought he knew every bird call and every animal vocalisation without even having to see the species. The area was alive with wildlife. Rustling trees and thick bushes hid the chirping of a plethora of birds, while thick bushes sheltered buzzing, ticking and snapping insects. But this sound was unfamiliar. He followed the resonance. When it stopped, a strange 'Woo Hoo, who hoo,' filled the air. It reminded him of a barn owl.

He froze. His mind jumped to one hot summer when he and Liz had often slipped out at night and had used it as a calling signal to let the other know they were there. His eyes scanned the flora. It couldn't be her, could it?

He spied his friend standing in a clearing. Like the last time, she appeared frightened and twitchy. And like every time, she was too far away for him to touch her.

He opened his mouth to call her name, but using sign language she frantically urged him to stop.

He stared at her face, his brow furrowing with confusion. She seemed even older than the last time he had seen her.

'What's happening to you?' he signed back. 'Why are you ageing so fast?'

She ignored his question and asked her own. 'How long have you been here, in India, Miles?'

His brow furrowed. He emitted an incredulous laugh. 'What a strange question. Four years. You know that.' He watched her head tilt upwards, the way she had always done when she assessed mathematical problems at school.

'Miles, you are in danger!' She signalled. 'You must escape. This forest is not what it seems.'

He flashed her his most charismatic smile. 'Liz, I'm fine,' he shouted towards her. 'Come here. I can help you.' He noted irritation etched onto her face.

'It's you that needs the help,' she signed. 'I believe they keep you subdued through drugs in the food. Miles, please! Don't eat or drink anything you haven't prepared yourself. You are running out of time. If you don't leave in the next forty days of your time, it'll be too late.'

Her head darted to the left. She stared at him one last time, her eyes wide with fear. 'They've found me!' Without saying goodbye, she sprinted through the foliage. Miles tried to follow her trajectory, but like all the times before, a heavy mist rolled in and obliterated his view.

Forty days of his time? He shook his head. What was she talking about?

When he woke up, he found himself in the clearing, on the picnic blanket, under the sun's rays, with no recollection of how he got there.

Geoff sat beside him, sipping champagne from the bottle and staring up at the sun. 'I can't believe we've been here five years already. Where has the time gone, eh?'

Confused, Miles sat up and rubbed his eyes. 'Sorry, what?'

'Us. We've been here five years already. Can you believe that? Where does the time go, huh?'

'You mean four years, don't you?'

'Nope! Wake up, sleepyhead. We've been here five years today!'

His words not only startled Miles, but jogged his memory.

'Listen, Geoff. I have to tell you something, but keep it to yourself, okay?' he didn't wait for a reply.

'I saw Liz again in the undergrowth this morning.' *At least I think it was this morning!*

He watched Geoff's eyes narrow. 'She told me the forest was dangerous and I must escape. I'm beginning to think she's right. Geoff, you should leave too.'

'What are you talking about?' Geoff emitted an incredulous laugh. 'I've been with you all morning. Listen, believe me. You never saw Liz. You've been dreaming, mate. That never happened.'

Mile's brow creased in confusion. 'No, I...'

Geoff laughed. 'Hell, I think you're losing it! Why would Liz still be in the forest after five years? That's ridiculous! Where would she live? What would she eat? And if the forest is as dangerous as she says, then why is she still here?'

Miles' frown deepened. He had a point. Why would she remain? But that didn't explain her rapid decline in her youthfulness. 'It's all so confusing. She's ageing so quickly, Geoff. It doesn't make any sense.'

'Maybe she's ill. I mean she doesn't sound mentally stable to me. Perhaps whatever debilitating disease she's suffering from has caused premature dementia. But I swear you haven't seen her today because I've been with you. I'd have seen her too.' He picked up the champagne bottle, took another swig, and waggled it under Miles' nose. 'I think you should drink more bubbly! It might stop giving you bad dreams!'

Miles laughed to pacify his friend, but he wasn't convinced. It felt like seconds ago he had stood in the middle of the forest and Liz had asked how long he had been there. He had said four years. Now Geoff was saying they had been there for five. How could he have lost a year?

Now he was in the clearing, but he didn't remember arriving. He had no recollection of eating lunch, drinking champagne, or falling asleep.

A flash of anxiety raged through his veins. What if Geoff was right, and he **had** imagined it all? Or worse still, his visions of Liz were not imaginary, and she had some weird degenerative illness. Perhaps it was somehow contagious, and she had infected him too!

'Come on, let's get back,' Geoff said, packing up the picnic basket. 'The girls will wonder where we are.'

The thought of never seeing Bella again urged Miles into action. 'You're right. Come on, let's go back to the hotel. I need to see my wife.'

Geoff smiled and patted Miles on the shoulder. 'Whatever you say, mate. Come on. Let's get you back to Bella and Shadow.'

'Shadow?'

'Jesus, Miles. You're seriously losing it! Shadow! Your three-year-old son. How can you not remember him? You've even brought him to the forest with us on occasion.'

As Geoff spoke, Miles pictured his son. He could remember his face and their time together, and he also remembered that Bella was pregnant.

Again!

Worry made his stomach clench. Maybe he was losing his mind. The numbers and dates just didn't add up.

'You need to go home and rest.' Geoff patted him on the shoulder.

Miles nodded. Perhaps Geoff was right. He needed a break from the forest. He should go home to Bella. He was safe with her. She would protect him.

'So, it's all decided,' Bell said with a nod.

'Huh? Sorry. What?' Miles took in his surroundings and realised they were sitting at a table in the tiny bar.

'I told you about your graduation ceremony,' Bella said with a sigh. She rubbed her swollen stomach, only days away from giving birth. 'Honestly. I swear you never listen to a word I say!'

'I do. Honest! I was just thinking about… well, how odd. I can't remember now. Sorry, Bella. Tell me again.'

'Your university in England has agreed that you and Geoff should remain here and continue your important research. They will allow you to attend the graduation ceremony online.'

'My graduation, yes.' His mind, muddy with a confusion of thoughts, fought to concentrate.

'Your parents will be in attendance. So, you will see them at the same time.'

'My parents, yes.' He didn't dare to admit he couldn't remember the last time he had even thought about his family. 'What about my brother?'

Bella frowned... 'He'll be there too,' she replied.

'What about Geoff?' he said, seeking him out among the rabble of people stuffed into the tiny room.

'Of course, he'll be there!' She shook her head in exasperation. 'You're graduating together, remember?'

'Er, yeah.' Mile squinted. Out of his peripheral view, he thought he glimpsed Geoff sitting in the corner, but when he focused, the face blurred until it looked nothing like him. Miles watched another bar patron heading toward the unfamiliar face and sitting down.

It was Miles's turn to furrow his brow.

'What's the matter now?' Bella said, rapidly losing her patience.

He focused on the man in the corner. His face remained the same, which just confused him even more. The longer he watched, the more pairs of eyes seemed to monitor him. He felt uncomfortable, but didn't want to admit it to Bella. As her pregnancy progressed, she seemed to get more and more cranky every day.

'Let's go home, Bella,' he said. 'I'm tired. I've had enough for tonight.'

Unable to hide her growing frustration, Bella sighed and pushed herself up from the table. 'I went to all this trouble to arrange the degree ceremony online so you wouldn't have all the hassle of travelling back to the UK and this is the thanks I get. You can't even say thank you?'

'Thank you, Bella. Of course, I'm grateful.' He lifted his beer and clinked her lemonade glass. 'To the most beautiful woman in the world. Cheers, and thank you!'

Her face softened slightly. She tapped her glass with his and gave him her most demure smile.

Miles returned it, but, for the second time, he experienced a tinge of discomfort. The air felt paused in anticipation, holding its breath, waiting for something huge to happen. But what?

The clientele in the tiny bar looked away as he perused them, almost afraid to make eye contact. Only the old barman made eye contact. He stood drying glasses with a dirty frayed cloth. His eyes seemed to bore into Miles' soul.

'Get out!' the force of his unspoken words pierced Miles' thoughts and filled his body with shock waves of fear.

Bella sensed his discomfort. 'Come. I'm tired. I agree with you. I think it's time we went back to the hotel.'

Miles didn't need to be told twice. The entire occupants of the bar were listening to the conversation. He wanted the floor to swallow him up. 'Very well,' he said, jumping to his feet.

His eyes glanced across at the table in the corner.

Geoff smiled and waved him goodbye.

Miles returned the salutation. But he was more confused than ever. When had Geoff sat down? And where was the man who was sitting there before him?

The entire village came out to see Miles and Geoff graduate. Not one to relish the spotlight, Miles had thrown up twice that morning due to nerves and the thought of being the centre of attention at the ceremony, both on-screen and off.

It wasn't the experience he had anticipated when he came to India. He'd expected to stay maybe six months, do his research and return to the UK to a formal graduation ceremony at the university. Instead, here he was, wearing his ceremonial robes, waiting in the town square to log on and graduate through cyberspace technology. A huge wide-screen TV dominated the little square so that everyone could watch the proceedings.

Geoff stood beside him, grinning like he'd won the lottery. Miles felt that, in a way, they both had. They had married beautiful young women who catered to their every need, and time slipped by in a haze of happiness.

The Dean appeared on the screen welcoming all graduates, their families and friends to the event. An orchestra played in the background. The university flag hung in the background behind him and the other seated faculty members. A podium on the right-hand side of the stage protected the speaker who announced the degree recipients one by one.

As Miles and Geoff were doctorate recipients, they were one of the first to be named. The camera swung back to the Dean.

'Our two botanists are currently working out in India and are attending this ceremony online. Hello, guys, can you hear and see me?'

Miles smiled into his computer screen. 'Yes, sir, we can.'

'Congratulations on your doctorates and on the amazing work you are achieving out there in India.' He turned to the audience. ' As I'm sure you know. These guys are world-renowned for their discoveries into eternal youth. Congratulations, both of you! You must be extremely proud of your accomplishments, as are we!'

'Thank you, sir. We couldn't be happier.' Miles replied as Geoff gave a thumbs up to the camera screen.

'Great, great! We have your families here.'

The camera panned around to his parents and his brother.

'Hello, Miles. Well done, son!' His father said, while his mother and brother waved at either side of him.

'Well done! We're so proud of you!' His mother grinned.

Miles smiled from ear to ear. 'Thank you! Miss you!'

'Nice one bro! Great job!' His brother yelled.

Miles' growing grin, slid from his face. A primal fear, so strong that he could hardly breathe overtook him. The colour fled his face, and he stared at the screen in disbelief.

His brother was deaf and non-vocal. It would be impossible for him to shout his congratulations.

The camera spun around to Geoff's family. The focus was on him, and Miles took that time to collect himself. Liz's words of warning rang through his brain.

*It's you who is in danger. It's in the food. You must escape!*

Was it true? Was he trapped in another world? It sounded too ridiculous to be correct, but something was extremely wrong here. Evil and foetidness encased him. They wove their sinister dark spells around him, wrapping him in a tight embrace from which he could no longer escape. He was the proverbial fly caught in the spider's sticky web. But how could he escape?

He still couldn't account for his lost year. Just thinking about it sent frissons of fear coursing through his veins and alarm bells rang in his brain. His mind was in turmoil. Nothing made sense.

A thought made his lungs fight to breathe. How could there be a perfectly functioning Wi-Fi connection when it was non-existent when he first arrived at this backwoods village in the middle of nowhere? Was five years long enough for it to reach the back of beyond? That's if he had been there for five years. Cold globules of sweat mixed with fear travelled down his back. Afraid to freak out and denounce the villagers for the frauds they were, he swallowed his anxiety and played along.

He glanced over at Bella. She held his son, Shadow's hand, and rocked his baby daughter, Misty, with the other.

Behind her stood her parents. The matriarchs of the forest. Why would he think that? *Because it's true!* His inner voice yelled. *This is all a lie.* A farce in which he played the starring role – but for what purpose?

Bella's beautiful smile once again lulled him into a false sense of security. He doubted himself. Maybe he was ill. This could all be a dream and when he woke up, everything would make sense.

Bella's brow twitched. She saw the confusion on her husband's face. In an instant, she passed the children to her mother and hurried to his side.

'Miles, look at me. What's the matter?' Her eyes searched his face for an answer. Her hands, already fumbling inside her bag, searching for a bottle. Miles returned her gaze. He immediately felt safe and calm when he stared into her eyes. 'I guess I'm just tired, that's all.'

'That's probably it,' Bella uncorked the bottle. 'Here, take this. It will revive you and help you get through the celebration.'

On impulse, through force of habit, and forgetting Liz's warning, Miles swigged the concoction.

'Yes, the celebration,' he repeated, no longer aware of what the village was celebrating. He grabbed her hand. 'Come on, let's dance. It's been a long time since we've danced together.'

'What about the kids?' Bella laughed, allowing him to pull her into the group of jiving villagers.

'That's what your parents are for!' He laughed as he swung her around and they danced the night away.

## Chapter Five

Geoff met him at the entrance to the forest, with his twin sons hanging onto his trousers and scuffing their shoes in the dirt.

'Morning Geoff. I see you've brought the boys this morning.'

Geoff grinned. 'Yeah, the little beggars wouldn't take no for an answer.'

Mile smiled. He nodded at the security guard who ignored him. He stood in his usual stoic position, holding the rifle and never moving from his spot.

Eight-year-old Helielle and Winnore grinned when they saw him. 'Hello, Uncle Miles!'

'Hello, boys. Fancy seeing you here.'

'We're helping Dad,' Helielle said. A proud tilt of his chin showed his arrogant determination.

'And you,' Winnore said, hiding behind his dad.

'Let's go then,' Miles replied, nodding to the guard again as they stepped inside, and still receiving no feedback.

He knew the forest so well. He had traversed the paths and wandered into the undergrowth so many times, there wasn't an inch of ground he couldn't recognise. The only difference was that today, his head was clearer than it had been for as long as he could remember. Ever since the degree ceremony, Liz's advice had hung inside his brain like wet laundry, refusing to be compartmentalised. *Don't eat or drink anything you haven't prepared yourself. You are running out of time. If you don't leave in the next four years of your time, it'll be too late.*

He had only drunk water for the past few days. The only food he had eaten was whatever he had prepared himself, and now Liz's advice seemed more poignant than ever. Something was wrong here. He could feel it, sense the malevolence festering all around him like a seeping wound that refused to heal.

Tricking Bella into believing he had eaten or drunk whatever she offered him was a challenge, but the longer he refrained from swallowing what she served, the clearer his thoughts became.

The twins skipped in front of him. Helielle turned and stared at him through narrowed eyes. He didn't speak, and his silence was more menacing than any words.

'Where are you going?' Winnore stopped walking. He blocked Mile's path and copied Helielle's stare.

'To look for specimens, of course. Like always.' He forced a smile. He sensed Geoff's presence close behind him.

He wondered if he was about to be attacked. The world felt wrong, off-kilter, as if it had somehow tipped off its axis and he was clinging on to some juxtaposed existence.

'Boys, stop questioning Uncle Miles. Let him get on with his work.'

Miles took off, striding through the undergrowth to get as far away from the trio as possible. Last night, when he had replayed the events of the degree ceremony, he had recognised another deceptive fact.

He had met Geoff's parents in the UK. The two people on the screen looked nothing like them! He now doubted Geoff was who he said he was. It seemed the only person he could trust was Liz, but everyone else told him she didn't exist.

Once he knew he was alone, he relaxed a little. He searched the undergrowth, only this time not for plants. Now he was looking for Liz.

In the distance, he heard Woo hoo, woo, hoo. After checking he wasn't being followed, he quickened his pace, responding to the sound edging closer. When he no longer received a reply, he assumed he was near. He dropped to his knees, looking for clues.

Suddenly, before him on the forest floor, he gasped with surprise. He had encountered a stout pair of fawn walking shoes peeking through the foliage. He slowly stood upright, following the legs upwards to a sturdy chest. He gasped when he recognised Liz's face. She had aged even more since the last time he had seen her.

'Liz? What's happened to you? I can help you. I've created the greatest potion to stop ageing. You should try it.' He reached out to touch her, but she held up her hands, halting him.

She swiped errant tears from her cheeks. 'Miles, listen. There isn't much time. You must leave this place. It's not what you think.'

'Liz,' he shook his head. Seeing her so deteriorated weakened his resolve. What if Geoff was right after all and he was slowly losing his mind? 'Are you ill? What's happened to you?'

'Don't talk. Just listen.' Her eyes darted left and right in fear of being discovered. 'You are trapped here. Nothing is what it seems.'

'Liz. You shouldn't be out here alone. Come with me. I'll get you some help.' He reached for her hand a second time.

She stepped further away. Her voice rose in anger. 'You are the one alone out here. It's you who needs help. Time is running out. You must leave now. Otherwise, it'll be too late.'

Miles frowned. 'Just tell me one thing. Tell me why you've aged in so little time. Please, Liz, I'm worried about you.'

The older botanist's shoulders sagged. 'Because what has been five years for you has been fifty years for me.'

Miles shook his head. 'What? That doesn't make sense.

'Think, Miles. Think back to that first morning in the forest. You did exactly what the barman told us not to do. You stepped off the path.'

'I...?'

'You were so excited you ran into the undergrowth to look at a specimen. Do you remember?'

Miles thought back through his fuzzy brain to that first morning. 'Yeah, I remember, but so what?'

'From the moment you stepped off the pathway, you disappeared. I've been looking for you ever since.'

'No, that's not right. I turned around and you and Geoff had disappeared. Then you jumped up. You were both laughing.'

'That wasn't me, Miles, and it wasn't Geoff either.'

'But you came back to the hotel with me and the next morning you had gone. You left me a note.'

Liz shook her head. 'No, Miles, that didn't happen. Do you think I'm that shallow I'd have left after spending the night with you the day before? I was in love with you. I've always loved you. Why do you think I've kept coming back time and time again to help you?'

Miles didn't speak. He couldn't. His mind was in turmoil. But Liz's words made sense. If what she said was true, it would explain her age. He suddenly felt trapped and alone in an unknown world. He gasped. 'So you're saying Geoff isn't who I think he is?'

Liz nodded. 'He left India when I did. We searched for two weeks for you. You simply disappeared. I've come back intermittently when the government has permitted me to do research, but the only reason I returned was to find you and warn you.'

Miles stared at her in disbelief. How could this be true?

'I've researched this forest and its myths and legends for years. It is inhabited by a species of evil faerie folk who can morph into the beholder's most beautiful desires and dreams. Everything you eat and drink is impregnated with herbs to keep you in a docile and drugged state. They are studying you as a species to strengthen themselves and become more impervious to outside danger. But believe me, Miles. Your entire existence there is a dream.'

He shook his head, refusing to believe it. 'No. I'm married. I have two children, and I've just graduated.' His brow furrowed. Rage bubbled in his veins. He turned angry eyes in her direction. 'No, it's not true! You are jealous. That's what it is. You envy my life and my success. You can't tell me my whole life has been a dream.'

Liz sighed. 'Not a dream, Miles, just a different time contingency.' She sighed and hung her head. It hurt her to break it to him like this. 'The truth is that Geoff and I graduated nearly forty years ago, Miles. We've had our careers and are now retired. Listen. This is the last time I can come to warn you. Get out before they overwhelm you forever. Accept the helping hand.'

Miles frowned. 'What's that supposed to mean?'

Liz gasped. Her eyes flicked to the left. 'They know I'm here. I have to go. Look for the man from the bar. Good luck.' She blew him a kiss, with tears streaming down her aged face. Then she took off as fast as she could through the forest.

'But, how? How do I get out?' His words echoed around him as he sank to his knees. Silence was his only reply. He sank to the forest floor, overcome by memories of his time in India and all the things that didn't make sense. How could he have had a video link to the University when he'd abandoned his phone on arrival because no signal existed there? How could he have become world renowned for his discovery if he'd never left the village and never once undergone an interview or been approached by the leading pharmaceutical companies?

Yet something still told him Liz's claims were fantastical. What if she was the one living in a different time frame and he was living in real time? He said it, but he didn't quite believe it. Too many things didn't add up in his world.

He recalled the night in the bar when Geoff's face had changed into someone else. The faerie folk probably exchanged personas with each other all the time. He became overwhelmed with sickness. Had Bella always been Bella, or had he been having sex with several different beings and impregnating them to produce stronger fae?

If Liz's previous warning had been correct, then his so-called wife was drugging him. Every morning she insisted he drank a special mineral juice. That, he now realised was to keep him subdued! Probably all the villagers were in on it. Perhaps they were all these species of warped, evil faerie beings, and he had fallen for their tricks time after time, year after year. He thumped himself repeatedly on his forehead.

His mind wandered back to his wedding ceremony when he discovered Bella's full name for the first time.

*'Do you, Bella Donna Nadaar take this man...'* Now he saw it for what it was (Belladonna). Her name was pure poison! And Nadaar was an Indian God with the body of a serpentine! He remembered reading about it before he had left England.

*My God, what am I doing here?* His fingers dug into the earth. He held up two fistfuls of black soil above his head. It could have been an expression of triumph, but his was pure rage.

A rustling behind him dragged him to the present.

'What are you doing? Why are you sitting on the floor?' Helielle asked. His tone was abrasive and confrontational. His eyes were like slits in his face. He blinked. Like a lizard, a third eyelid flicked across his eye.

Miles' stomach contracted. He registered the hatred in the child's eyes. He may be young, but his anger was already evident. Who knew? Whoever or whatever was in front of him might not be a kid at all, but a faerie adult marauding as a child. The only thing he knew for sure was that whatever stood before him radiated evil.

More rustling through the undergrowth signalled Winnore's arrival. He also exuded a palpable malevolence.

'Hey, Winnore,' Miles feigned nonchalance.

The children, if that's what they truly were, stood shoulder to shoulder, monitoring him like he was part of a laboratory experiment.

'What're you doing over here, boys? Where's your dad?'

When they didn't reply, he feigned ignorance to their threatening manner. He beckoned them towards him.

'Helielle, come and look at this.' He pointed to a plant. 'This is the reason I'm sitting on the ground. This plant is called Uginel. It has healing properties, and it is extremely rare to find it.'

He waited for some response that wasn't forthcoming. He still sensed the nefariousness of their stance but was determined not to show his growing inquietude. 'Winnore, can you pass me my small shovel, please?'

When the boy passed it over, Helielle grabbed Miles' wrist.

'You can't dig it up. Have you learnt nothing in all the time you've spent here? You mustn't remove anything from the forest.'

Miles shrugged him free. 'Don't you think I know that? I'm not digging it up, Helielle. I'm clearing the weeds around it so that it can thrive.'

'BOYS! Where are you?' Geoff's voice echoed through the trees. His footsteps through the undergrowth announced his approach.

'They're over here, Geoff. With me.'

Geoff, or the being he had always considered to be Geoff, crashed through the shrubbery.

'Hi!' He stood with both hands on his hips, taking in the situation. 'Shall we go eat? I'm starving. I don't know about you.'

Glad to get the chance to stand up and gain superiority over the boys, Miles agreed.

'Sounds good to me. Lead the way!' He hoped his voice held a joviality that he wasn't feeling.

As they walked, Miles realised he had put himself between the malevolent faeries. He didn't like it. The boys were in front. Geoff was at the rear.

They walked in silence to the clearing. The picnic blanket and basket were laid out, as usual, but it was only then Miles questioned their existence. Who brought the food every day? Why had he never bothered to question it before?

He slumped onto the blanket. He knew the answer.

Before, when he'd swallowed Bella's "fruit juice" drink without question, or anything else she'd given him to ingest, he'd lived in a false state of euphoria and questioned nothing.

Now, he was waking up after what felt like forever. His sluggish brain was returning to its rapier-like form. He finally recognised and accepted what Liz had said was true. Something was majorly wrong and malevolently twisted in the forest.

Correction. Not just in the forest. Everywhere! In the entire village!

He began to question everything.

How could he have a top-notch laboratory in such a tiny village, in the back of beyond that screamed of poverty? How had he not thought of that before?

Why was he still living in a hotel when he was married with children? His stomach clenched, thinking about it.

A primal urge to escape set every never-ending alight. His thoughts fled to Liz. She had spent her life trying to help him. She had begged him to escape. But was that even possible?

Winnore broke into his thoughts. 'Here, Uncle Miles', it's one of your favourites. A salad sandwich!'

Miles blinked. He fought not to flinch and draw back with repulsion. Between two pieces of bread, bugs of all shapes and sizes undulated and crawled over each other. Some fell from the sandwich onto the blanket. He fought the urge not to scream. His thoughts went back to all the times he had reached for his favourite sandwich and remarked how the contents were so plentiful they almost fell out from between the bread. Now, he realised they had fallen out. Bugs by the bucket load dropped onto the blanket and crawled, slithered and skittered across his lap.

'Thanks, Winnore, but not today. I'm not hungry.'

Out of the corner of his eye, he watched Helielle shoot out a long, thin, green tongue. It flicked up a bug, and he swallowed it whole.

Miles could hardly comprehend what he had witnessed. Every atom of his being cried out for him to flee, but he knew he had to act and do what he usually did.

Pretending to be tired, he laid back on the blanket with both hands behind his head. 'Ah!' he exclaimed. 'This is the life, isn't it, Geoff? Good food, wine and company in the most beautiful place in the entire world.'

Geoff poured two glasses of champagne. 'Here,' he pushed a glass towards him. 'Cheers!'

Miles took the glass, but had no intention of swallowing the liquid. For all he knew, it could be poisonous tree sap! Anything to put him back into a false sense of euphoria.

'Cheers.' He clinked glasses and then pretended to drink. He laid down again, placing the glass on the grass, but keeping hold of it. His eyes almost closed, but he could still see from under his lashes. He saw Geoff and the boys, tick-tacking between them. Assuming the champagne had put him to sleep, they clicked and hissed, in an unknown language. They seemed to argue and give each other orders.

Miles had never felt so alienated, alone and afraid. He could hardly move. He dared himself to tip the glass centimetre by centimetre, releasing the tainted champagne into the grass while their focus was on each other.

He continued to study them through slits in his eyelids. When Helielle's facial image smudged into a blur of green skin, patchy ginger hair, pointed ears and cold almond-shaped eyes, Miles' gasp caught in his throat. Aware his entire body had tensed, he forced himself to relax.

Three pairs of almond eyes monitored him in silence.

He exhaled as though he were sleeping. Then rolled onto his side, facing them.

They studied him for a few moments before continuing their angry chittering.

He wanted to jump up and bolt for the undergrowth. What hellish nightmare was he caught up in? All three of them had reverted into other beings. Miles was terrified. He didn't know if they were faerie folk, aliens from another planet or what they were. There was only one thing he felt sure to be the truth. One wrong move and they'd kill him.

The bar owner's words from Miles' first night in India came back to haunt him. *'Many men enter but few return.'* He cringed at the thought. What category was his destiny?

Behind the three beings, he spotted movement. The old barman from Miles' first night in India was hiding in the undergrowth. His clothes were dishevelled, old and torn. Unkempt, thin locks of hair hung long and ragged like his scraggly beard. His skin was dark and leathery, his extremities were thin and gangly. He caught Mile's eye, held out one hand and beckoned him to join him.

The botanist felt strangely calmed, as though he could sense the man's true soul. Then he froze. How could he know if this was a trick? What if the guy could transform into another faerie-like being, and his fate would be in their hands? Determined to play it safe, he had to continue doing what he had always done. That meant pretending to sleep.

'Miles, wake up,' Geoff shook him "awake" even though he hadn't closed his eyes properly at all.
'The boys are getting restless. Would you mind if we went home early?'

'Of course not. Come on, let's go.' This was better than he had expected. The sooner he could escape their clutches the sooner he could work out what to do next.

As usual, they left the picnic basket where they found it.

For the first time, Miles wondered when it was replenished. The answer seemed unimportant. The truth was, he now knew he hadn't been eating all his favourite things. That was just another illusion.

They strode in silence to the forest entrance. Once again, Miles was flanked by Geoff and his sons. Only the swish of the leaves and flick of grass broke the escalating silence. When Mile spied the gates and the open road ahead, he had to fight not to break into a run.

Two Tuk-Tuks stood waiting, their engines running. How did they know he'd be leaving at that time? Why were the vehicles there at all? They usually walked back to the hotel. What made today any different?

He headed for the first one, walking quicker than he intended.

Helielle veered toward him, breaking into a trot to catch him up.

The botanist guessed the boy didn't trust him and intended to shadow him. Miles had no intention of giving Helielle the opportunity. He jumped into the Tuc-Tuc and ordered the driver to go.

'Get in with your father,' Miles shouted. 'I have things to do.'

Helielle stopped. He glared at Miles, his hands converting into fists.

Miles glanced backwards. The trio followed close behind in the second vehicle. They sat in silence, just staring in his direction.

'Will this go any faster?' he asked the driver.

'No, sir, this is top speed.'

Miles gripped the seat in frustration. He couldn't lose them at this rate. He wanted to grab the driver by the shoulders and demand to know if he was part of the farce he now called his life. He chanced another look behind. The two boys blurred out of focus. He saw the greenish tinge of the faerie skin, the almond-shaped eyes that gave him the creeps, and their augmenting rage that seemed to radiate from them in a haze of red.

When he reached the hotel, he jumped out of the moving tuk-tuk and raced inside, calling Bella's name. He intended to grab her, force her to tell him what she had done and demand she tell him how to get out of this living nightmare.

The door to his room stood open, but Bella and all her belongings were gone. Another glitch before his eyes left him light-headed as the room shifted. He now stood in the original room he had stayed in that first night in India. The night Liz had knocked on his door. Only now the feeling of decay was a thousand times worse. The walls ran thick with spores of dark-green mould that clung to the walls, twisted in thick stringy lines. The air was thick and damp. He couldn't breathe.

'BELLA!' he shouted. His building anger curled one hand into a fist and he punched the wall, leaving his imprint in the crumbling remains.

'Where are you?' He ran back to the reception area.

The front desk was devoid of personnel. A thick layer of dust covered everything. The foyer had been ransacked. Broken remains of aged rotting furniture and overturned planters with long dead shrubs lay strewn across the tattered carpet. His mind registered what he was seeing, but he couldn't bring himself to believe it. Spooked, he ran down the corridor, wading through dirty brown water that lined the floors and splashed around his ankles.

Then he saw him.

Sitting on the long stone steps, was his son.

'Shadow,' he cried, relieved to have found him.

The child looked toward him with deadened eyes. A sliver of skin fell like cascading sugar from his face. Miles cried out in disbelief when his child slumped, then crumbled into dust. The scattered ashes fell into the dirty, rippling water and were carried away.

All Miles' hopes and dreams went with it.

'NO!' His pain echoed around the corridor. He collapsed to his knees, tears coursed down his cheeks and a primeval roar like a wounded animal burst from his core.

A burning rage surged through his veins. 'BELLA!'

His voice bounced off the empty wall.

A stillness descended. The building seemed paused, waiting for him to make his next move.

He spun around.

Geoff and the boys stood blocking his exit. They didn't even try to disguise their true identities.

'Bella is waiting for you. You only need to come with us,' Geoff replied, edging closer.

'Stay away from me. All of you. Whatever you are!'

'Miles, you're having a nervous breakdown. You haven't been taking your medicine. Come with us. Bella is waiting for you, Miles. She's worried about you.'

Miles' eyes narrowed. 'I don't think so. That ain't gonna happen. Stay the hell away from me!'

His eyes searched the surrounding area for a weapon. He spied a metal pipe leaning up against the wall and grabbed it. He swung it like a deranged giant, hell-bent on destruction. 'None of this is real. You've tricked me! But I'm on to you. It's too late and I'm getting out of here. Move out of my way.'

The being called Geoff smiled. A supercilious grin that made Miles want to bash his head in with the pipe.

'You're too late,' he said, edging closer. His sons matched him step by step. 'You've missed the deadline. Your little friend Liz wasn't vigilant enough. She got her calculations wrong. Now, you'll never get out.'

Miles turned and ran. He splashed through the water and charged down the corridor; the trio closing the gap behind him. When he turned the corner, he spied an aperture where a window used to be. He threw himself through and landed in an ungainly heap on the dusty ground outside.

He recognised the same scruffy kids from his first day, but this time their skin had a greenish hue, and their almond-shaped eyes held a sinister gleam as they rushed towards him.

Miles knew he had to get back to the forest. The old man who had held out his hand was his salvation. He realised now that the infinity he had felt the first time he had seen him was what Liz referred to.

She had said the eyes were the window to the soul. He had looked into the vagabond's eyes and seen humility. That was something that Miles had lost a long time ago but hadn't realised it. His visions of plant and specimen searches, writing academic papers and becoming world-renowned were all just fantasies. He had accomplished nothing. He was trapped in the matrix, an imaginary world where nothing was real, and evil outweighed goodness a thousand to one.

With several of the faerie beings in pursuit, he clutched the lead pipe, jumped into a Tuk-Tuk and caught his breath as it sped back to the forest. He soon lost it again when he looked behind him. The beings were flying! In a V formation, they pursued the vehicle. Their spindly arms now had membranes attached to their sides. Stick-like legs dangled as they flew, reminding him of oversized bats. Their incessant chittering filled the sky, but their eyes remained focused on Miles and his escape.

As the Tuk-Tuk travelled along the edge of the market. Miles saw his chance. He threw himself from the vehicle, rolled towards the stalls and emerged on the other side into the hustle and bustle of shoppers, looking for a bargain.

He kept his head bowed and his shoulders hunched, hoping not to draw attention to himself. Miles didn't know where he was going, or what he wanted to do. His main goal was to lose his adversaries.

The villagers appeared oblivious to his existence and, for a moment; he forgot they were all in this together. Then he found his trajectory slowing down. The villagers surged toward him, forcing him backwards. Suddenly, someone pulled his arm.

'Miles? What are you doing here? I thought you'd still be in the forest?'

Bella flashed him her heartwarming smile. It melted his heart. For a few seconds, he debated that this could all be a dream. Maybe he was having a nervous breakdown and none of this was real.

'Here, try this plum. They're the first of the season, and so juicy!'

She reminded him of a wicked witch with a shiny pristine apple in her wizened hand. He looked down, his eyes blinked at the fat grub she held between her fingers.

'NO!' he batted it from her fingers.

'Ow! What's the matter with you?'

He grabbed her by the shoulders and peered into her eyes. Where once he had seen ecstasy, true happiness and contentment, now he witnessed emptiness, blackness and decay.

'You can't trick me anymore, Bella.'

Her brow creased. 'What are you talking about? Do you feel okay? Let's go back to the hotel.'

'I've just come from there, Bella. I've seen how we are living. You have deceived me. You've had me fooled for years, but this is it. The end. Goodbye!' He pushed her away and forced his way through the swarms of people.

'Miles, wait!' Her voice drifted to him through the crowd. The oppressive confusion of bodies parted to form a tunnel of bodies between them for Bella to reach him. Miles didn't look back. He sprinted to the edge of the market, flagged down another Tuk-Tuk, and headed for the forest.

Miles raced towards the main entrance. The guard stood in his usual stoic position.

Despite his hurry to escape, Miles realised that apart from the first few days, he had never seen the guy move. He always adopted the same stance: his legs apart, both hands on his rifle and thick mirrored shades over his eyes.

Intrigued, Miles approached with caution. He looked for signs of life. A heaving chest or a single bead of sweat on his solemn face. Anything. Getting no reaction, Miles raised his index finger and prodded him on the shoulder. The soldier's entire frame wobbled before falling back into place. Miles stood in front of him. And lunged forward as if to hit him.

The soldier still didn't react.

Shocked, Miles grabbed the mirrored glasses with both hands and snatched them from his face. A gasp escaped his lips.

A shop mannequin stared back at him.

Emitting a bellow of fury and frustration. He thumped the shop dummy in the chest. It fell, almost in slow motion, to the ground. Miles' fingers curled into fists again. Rage soared from his stomach and escaped through his vocal cords in a deadly roar. The sound urged him forward. He charged into the forest, desperately searching for the old man.

The atmosphere, once bright, warm and welcoming was dank and cold. The absence of the usual sounds of birds calling to each other, rabbits and deer foraging in the undergrowth filled him with dread. In their place, all things dark and creepy slithered and crawled along the forest floor and hid in the trees. Huge arachnids spun humongous webs, poisonous toads hopped across his feet, and different species of enormous snakes, known as "The Big Four" curled around his legs. The buzz of millions of insects only heightened his fear. They nipped at his exposed skin and sucked his blood. He slapped them away, but they refused to leave.

The damp grey mist slid through the trees and headed toward him. Was its purpose to slow him down, confuse him, and force him in another direction? He had no intention of taking a diversion. He knew where he had to go.

He reached the clearing where he always ate lunch, but now, he hardly recognised it. Gone was the short grass, pleasant atmosphere and beautiful sunlight to warm his bones. Now it stood in darkness. The cold seeped under his skin, chilling his bones. The rolling grey mist surged toward him like a tsunami wave, encompassing him in its chilly embrace.

The Naja-naja or Speckled Cobras hissed a greeting from the branches of the trees. Huge specimens of Echis Carinatus and Bungarus Caeruleus, more commonly known as the saw-scaled viper and the common krait, slithered toward him in the long grass.

He forged onward, wading through the overgrown, razor-sharp grass. The sticky blades sliced into his forearms. He heard the now familiar chittering of whispering Fey. Miles knew they surrounded him but, determined to escape, he surged forward.

As if his hearing had intensified, he heard arrows plucked from ancient quivers. They fired toward him in an almost choreographed display of precision.

He ducked and twisted, jumped and crawled, but the projectiles penetrated his skin, their poison oozed under his epidermis. He felt himself weakening.

As he reached the end of the clearing. The old barman stepped out from behind a thick tree trunk into his view. He stood in silence, a few paces away waiting for him, his hand outstretched.

Miles guessed the man was afraid to enter the clearing. He remained on the periphery. The botanist forged ahead. He stretched out his hand to the old man.

Another arrow lodged in the back of his neck, and he dropped to the ground. The old man held out his hand and curled his fingers, beckoning him, and urging him to crawl.

With a breath away from losing consciousness. Miles held out his hand.

The world turned black.

*

'Mile, Miles, can you hear me?'

He forced his eyes open, squinting into the brightness.

'Where am I?'

'You're in the hospital. You've been here several weeks.'

'What happened?'

'You collapsed in the forest, but don't worry. You're going to be fine now.'

'I've had the weirdest dream…'

'You've had me so worried, Miles. I thought I'd lost you.'

Miles stared into her eyes and smiled. He could see the worry etched on her face. Someone had once said the eyes were the window to the soul… he couldn't remember who it was, but he knew true love when he saw it.

'Don't worry. I'll never leave you.' He patted her hand.

'I know, that, Miles. I've always known that.' Bella smiled.

THE END

## REVIEWS

As a struggling writer,

I humbly ask of you,

To spare just a minute, please

And leave a short review.

Every comment written,

And every five-star rating

Helps me as a writer,

And is a cause for celebrating.

So, help a struggling author,

As then, my friend, you see,

What may seem unimportant,

Will mean the world to me.

Dear Reader,

The premise of this book came to me in a dream. It was so vivid; I had to grab a pen and paper and document what I had dreamed.

If you have enjoyed it, you may be interested in reading my paranormal horror novel **"Raven's Retreat"**. The novel is based on my home in the Spanish countryside, which is haunted.

Several of the events in the novel actually happened. I wonder if you can separate fact from fiction.

Here is the blurb and the First Chapter:

**BLURB:**

**Greed led them in. Destitution kept them there.**

Adam and Becky Hargreaves stumble upon a foreboding gothic-style property in the secluded Spanish countryside, and believe they've found the ideal business opportunity. But shortly after moving in with Nerea, their truculent teenager, Melissa, their baby daughter, and Rose, Becky's infirm mother, a series of disturbing events shatter their dreams of success.

When ghostly orbs and manifestations of the dead roam the corridors threatening their business and their lives, steadfast Adam refuses to believe their home is possessed. As he withdraws from his family, Becky and her sparring stepdaughter Nerea must learn to work together to solve the ulcerating secret lying in the dark heart of the house before history repeats itself.

What happened all those years ago during Franco's regime? Why are so many spirits of young children still wandering the halls of the retreat? And who or what evil being is keeping them there?

As rivers of blood run deep within the bowels of the property, the family finds themselves entangled in an age-old promise with the devil. Who can they trust? How can they discover what happened in the blood-chilling past before time runs out?

Only one family member will make it out alive. Who can outwit the black soul and his disciples lying in wait inside the walls of Raven's Retreat?

Dare you venture inside?

# CHAPTER ONE

## A Dream Come True
## Águilas, Murcia Spain

Becky swivelled around in a tight circle. Anxiety built as she scanned the vast, sun-baked, barren landscape. One hand shielded her eyes; the other on her hip.

'Where the hell is she?'

Adam half mimicked his wife's actions. One hand shaded his bright green eyes, the other clutched a baby carrier containing his six-month-old daughter, Melissa.

Apart from a few oddly placed trees pushing out of the hardened soil and stretching like deformed limbs towards the sun, he couldn't spy any sign of life. His hand lowered and switched the baby carrier into his other hand.

'I've no idea.'

'Well, she must be somewhere!' Becky's voice rose, highlighting her frustration tinged with worry. 'I mean, how can a seventy-year-old woman with Alzheimer's disappear?'

'She was here a minute ago.'

Becky sighed. Talk about stating the bleeding obvious! her inner-self screamed. 'We know that much, Adam! The question is. Where the hell is she now?'

Adam hitched the baby carrier into position to avoid the question. He twisted around to face his sixteen-year-old daughter. She was the mirror image of her father. Bright ginger hair, lean and athletic with the same vivid green eyes, whereas Melissa took after her mother with blue eyes and blonde hair.

'Did you see where she went, Nerea?'

The teenager, busy punching a message into her phone, raised her head, gracing him with a withering glance through phlegmatic eyes. 'Huh?' Boredom tinged with insolence radiated from her freckled-faced expression like penetrating gamma rays. '¡Yo que sé! Ni idea.' (I don't know. I've no idea).

Adam scowled. 'Put the phone away! We're supposed to be enjoying a day out together, but you're not here. You're too engrossed in your mobile.'

Nerea glared at her father before ramming the phone into the back pocket of her jeans. The thought of moving to Aguilas made her feel sick. She didn't want to leave her life in Almería.

The teenager bent down to pick up a stick and waggled it with little enthusiasm toward their dogs.

The two young black and white collies scampered around her. They jumped, barked, and bumped into each other in anticipation of the gnarled twig being thrown.

Adam detected Becky's annoyance level rising another notch at his daughter's insolence. He understood the underlying tension between the two females, but he hated it. Nerea had never truly accepted Becky. Adam's first wife, Candela, a Spanish native, had passed away when his daughter was just six years old. When Becky had come into their lives, He had viewed her as a Godsend. Someone who could pull him out of the depths of despair and someone willing to act as a mother figure for his daughter.

Nerea had viewed Becky as quite the opposite. An interloper; someone bent on penetrating the father/daughter relationship and leaving her floundering on the sidelines.

Adam emitted a deep sigh. He knew until he found his mother-in-law, Rose, he would continue to sense the negative emotions of his wife and oldest child in stereo. Some day out! He thought as he trudged behind his wife.

They had travelled from their home in Almería to the province of Murcia on a house-hunting expedition. After several unsuccessful viewings, Adam had cancelled the day's scheduled appointments and announced an excursion to the countryside. Now he was regretting it.

They continued walking north. The dogs, Hazel and Nuts, charged ahead, darting backwards and forwards, so full of youth and energy and oblivious to the rising tensions of their owners. Hazel got her name because of a small brown pattern on the tip of her nose, while Nuts lived up to his name. He was just crazy! He ran around in circles, trying to catch his tail, as though he had a rabid cat clasped to the end.

As their strides elongated, Becky and Adam called out Rose's name. Nerea made an occasional half-hearted contribution when she wasn't sending text messages. Several minutes later, with still no sign of Rose, the group came across a narrow dirt road with an abundance of flora lining both sides. Sturdy bushes, a myriad of wildflowers and towering trees all flourished under the Murcia sun and swayed with the gentle Levante breeze.

Despite her distress at losing her mother, the sheer abundance of flora struck Becky as odd. Their day trip to the countryside wasn't the lush, ardent landscape she had expected. Apart from a few lettuce fields and a line of dusty greenhouses, the entire area was arid, powdery, and barren.

'How odd to see all this greenery. It makes me think of the UK, rather than Southern Spain,' she said.

Adam had noticed it, too. 'Yeah, someone has got green fingers around here. Just look at this place. It's like an oasis in the desert.'

Nerea snorted. 'Maybe it's a mirage… or we're in the twilight zone!'

The two adults ignored her sarcasm.

Becky marched along the twisting pathway, impatient to find her mother. Adam plodded behind her, growing more disillusioned by the minute.

Nerea glanced in her father's direction, grabbed his hand and pulled him back. 'Should we go any further?' Her voice dropped to a whisper. 'I've got a nasty feeling about this. It's private property.'

'Maybe you're right, but I think when the owners discover our reason, they won't mind. After all, we've got a genuine reason for coming onto their land. We must find Rose.' He set off in long strides, hoping to catch up with Becky, but realising his daughter was lagging behind, he turned back, torn between the two females. 'Come on!' he urged, beckoning her forwards and waiting until she caught up. 'Put your phone away! I'm counting on you to do the talking. I'm not sure my Spanish is up to explaining all this.'

Nerea groaned and rolled her eyes heavenwards. She was used to being her father's unpaid, personal interpreter. She knew what was coming: He would push her forwards and stand in the background letting her deal with the situation. Sometimes she felt like she was the adult, and they were her children!

They followed the meandering pathway, which wound toward a cluster of mountains that dwarfed the fields below them. With every step, the foliage grew thicker and healthier. As the group rounded the next bend, they found themselves in a clearing. An imposing, weatherworn two-storey establishment sat at the foot of a mountain.

'What is this place?' Nerea whispered. She came to a stop, eyed the rundown building with scrutiny and shivered despite the sun. 'It gives me the creeps.'

A flock of black ravens perched at strategic positions along the sagging roof watched her in silence. They reminded her of an audacity of grotesque gargoyles.

Adam let out another long sigh. 'Let's just get this over with, shall we? As soon as we know Rose isn't here, we'll be on our way, okay?'

Nerea mirrored her father's exasperated release of breath. She hunched her shoulders, scuffing her trainers along the remaining gravel in the driveway. 'Okay, but please, not a moment longer. This place reminds me of those seventies horror films you love to watch!'

Adam grinned, then nudged her in the ribs. 'Forever the Drama Queen! Come on. You've got your brave, handsome father to protect you.'

Nerea groaned, gave him a wry smile tinged with sarcasm, and flicked her eyes heavenwards to express her annoyance at this unwelcomed diversion.

Father and daughter caught up with Becky as she reached toward the grotesque door knocker. It featured a rusting iron gargoyle holding a heavy ring between misshapen teeth. Its eyes blackened and dead appeared to be laughing at the three visitors. Becky's insides squirmed. Her hand was suddenly unwilling to touch the deathly cold metal ring.

'Go on.' Adam's impatience provoked more animosity between the couple.

Becky flashed him a withering look, snatched up the ring and banged it three times onto the thick wood. The knocking echoed inside the cavernous hallway, bouncing off the walls and traversing the corridors until it trailed to nothing.

Impatience built as they lingered on the porch for someone to open the double doors. As the minutes ticked by, Becky's anxiety levels soared. She tapped the knocker again, then drummed her thighs with open palms, swayed from one foot to the other, and let out an irritated click of her tongue. 'Come on. Hurry!'

When one of the imposing, heavy doors clicked open with an ominous groan, they found a tall, good-looking man around Adam's age standing before them.

'Yes?' He brushed his wayward fringe back into place amid the mass of blonde hair while he perused the group. His eyes stopped on Nerea, assessing her with an admiring grin.

'Oh, you speak English!' Becky's body relaxed as she flashed him a relieved smile.

Spooked, Nerea edged closer to her father and hung onto his arm.

'Er... sorry to bother you, but we seem to have misplaced my mother. She suffers from Alzheimer's. One minute she was there and the next she'd vanished!' Becky finished with an embarrassed laugh, ashamed of her ineptitude in taking care of her aged mother.

The owner grasped the door as though he needed it for support. He seemed lost for words, yet his eyes sparkled as though he was enjoying a private joke, and they were a part of it.

'Hello, I am Hans. Yes, I speak English, but my wife and I are Dutch.' He opened the door wider. 'Come in, come in! I think your search is over. I believe my wife has found your mother.'

'Ah!' Becky exhaled. Daring to believe her anxiety was about to end.

Hans pushed open the portal wide enough for the family to shuffle into the huge hallway. Their eyes gazed at the enormous, high ceiling and a huge, stained-glass window that reflected the sun. It created a dancing mirage of different coloured lights on the worn tiled floor. Their exclamations of amazement filled the open space. The sounds echoed off walls laden with framed portraits and hanging tapestries.

Becky marvelled at the sweeping staircase, which dominated the hallway of the house. The steps increased in size from the top to the bottom. The final few circled outwards, reminding her of a thick, glutinous liquid rippling downwards, spanning out across the floor.

Even Nerea seemed lost for words. She stared upwards at the balcony-style upper corridor with its host of closed doors dotted along it. An involuntary shiver made the hairs at the back of her neck stand on end. For all its grandeur, she sensed an uneasiness she couldn't quite explain.

'This way.' Their host held out an arm, and they followed him down a long, thin corridor that opened out into a spacious country kitchen. Worktops made of thick pinewood ran around three walls which were painted in a buttercup yellow. A polished Aga dominated the back wall. Crockery and utensils from the past lined the walls, adding to the room's country-kitchen vibe.

Becky sighed with relief when she spied her mother sitting at the large wooden table in the middle of the kitchen. Rose was chatting with the lady of the house like they were old friends. So animated was she and engrossed in the conversation, that Rose didn't even notice Becky's entrance.

'Amy, this is Rose's family. They've been searching for her,' Hans explained.

The woman rose slowly, then brushed two hands down the contours of her slim physique to straighten her clothes. She flicked back her long blonde hair with a swish of her head and fixed them all with a dazzling smile.

'Hello, nice to meet you all. Please, take a seat. You must be thirsty. Let me make you all a drink.'

'No, please, don't put yourself out!' Becky replied. 'I'm just relieved to have found my mother again. Thank you so much for taking her in.'

'I assure you, it's no trouble. Sit down. I'll make us all some lemonade. It's so hot out there. You can't go without at least taking a little refreshment.'

Becky pulled out a chair and sat next to her mother. 'Well, if you're sure that's okay. That'd be great!'

Nerea glared in Becky's direction, pulled out another chair so it scraped on the kitchen tiles, then slumped down into it; her arms folded across her chest in defiance. She had hoped to find Rose and leave. The place gave her the creeps, and Hans was even creepier. He reminded her of a 'Stepford husband'. He appeared robotic, his smile forced, and his movements controlled. Every time she caught his eye, he was assessing her like some sort of deranged pervert. She squirmed with embarrassment and discomfort before extracting her mobile again.

Becky ignored her stepdaughter's sullen expression and patted her mother's arm. 'You had me worried. You can't wander off like that!'

Rose squinted towards her through rheumy eyes, studying the face for a hint of recognition. Nothing was forthcoming.

Adam placed baby Melissa's carrier on the table, then stood with his hands on his hips, surveying the enormous kitchen. 'This is quite some place you've got here, er...' he glanced at his host, waiting for him to relinquish his name a second time.

'Hans. Yeah, it sure is.'

Amy handed out glasses of lemonade to the females but presented Adam with a wine glass brimming with what appeared to be rosé wine. 'Pardon me for presuming, but you look like you could do with something stronger.'

Adam took the glass and inspected the liquid, swirling it around in the glass.

The couple refrained from speaking. They stood straight and rigid, watching him with intense eyes, their fists clenched until he took the first sip.

'Hum, that's very nice. It's got an unusual taste...' It reminded him of something he couldn't quite place.

'Yes, it has. It's made here on the grounds.' The couple cast a sly smile at each other that Becky caught.

Adam held the glass out to her, but she shook her head.

'How long have you been living here?' he said, making conversation.

'Oh, a while,' Hans replied. 'It's a pity we've got to sell it.'

'Sell it? Why's that?'

'I'm afraid that, like yourselves, we have ageing parents, and a few days ago, we received some unwelcome news. Both my parents are ill. I'm sorry to say we need to return to Holland as soon as possible. In fact, we've just put the house on the market.'

Adam stared at Hans. His brain working overtime. Lucid visions of turning the place into a countryside bed-and-breakfast hotel or some sort of retreat flooded his thoughts. They had been searching for a similar property for almost two weeks. Had Rose inadvertently stumbled upon the ideal location? Adam took another sip of wine, becoming almost drunk with anticipation.

'We'll have to sell it at a low price, as we need to leave,' Hans said.

A smile broke across Adam's face, which he couldn't quite control. 'You might be in luck. We're house hunting right now. We're thinking about opening a small guest house. Is that what you were planning?'

He missed the flash of a sly smile between the couple.

'No. Far from it,' Hans replied.

'Although we've had our fair share of visitors,' his wife replied.

Becky registered that sly flash of a smile pass between the couple a second time.

Hans clapped his hands. 'We're nurses, you see. When we bought the property a few years ago, we applied for a licence to open a care home for the elderly. We thought it'd be an idyllic setting for them to live the rest of their lives in the peaceful setting of the Spanish countryside.' He stopped talking and eyed Adam like a farmer at a cattle market assessing a bull. 'Come,' he said, heading down the corridor. 'I'll give you a tour.'

Adam placed his empty glass on the table and sprinted after Hans, leaving the girls alone in the kitchen.

Nerea realised that a quick exit from this weird old house was now a long-forgotten dream. In a moment of pent-up emotion, she banged her glass down on the kitchen table.

The women gasped as the tumbler exploded and one sliver of glass sliced into the angry teenager's hand with surgical precision.

Baby Melissa jumped and started to cry.

'Oh, my God! I'm so sorry!' Becky jumped up, unsure which child to comfort first.

With a flick of her hand, Amy motioned she'd attend to Nerea. 'These things happen. Don't worry.' She grabbed a clean cloth to cover the cut on the teen's hand and used another to wipe the scarred wooden table.

Becky gave Amy an apologetic smile. 'I'm sorry about my husband dragging Hans away like that. Adam's a real dreamer. He's always making these rash decisions. I'm sure he's just wasting your husband's time. I don't think we could afford such an enormous property.'

Amy watched with a hint of fascination as Nerea sucked blood from her hand. She heard Becky's comments, but they didn't register. Amy shook her head as though to clear her thoughts.

'Sorry. What?'

'I said, I don't think we'd be able to afford it,' Becky replied.

The woman returned Becky's apologetic smile with a crafty grin. 'You never know. Stranger things have happened. You may be surprised.'

***

Six months later: Moving Day

A car trundled through the open front gates, disturbing the virtual silence of the countryside. It traversed the uneven, slightly tilting, potholed access, coming to an abrupt stop ten metres from the threshold. In the surrounding trees, the army of ravens shuffled closer together. Shoulder to shoulder, their eyes flicked and flashed. Their wings twitched and fluttered. They gargled in muttered communication, observing the family's arrival with guileful interest.

The house loomed before the newcomers; a cumbersome, mismatched, two-story edifice. Multifarious windows blinked in the sunlight like a myriad of eyes, assessing the emerging occupants of the car.

The family returned the gaze as they exited the vehicle, one by one. Becky retrieved Melissa from the back seat and transferred her to the baby carrier. The others stretched and yawned, attempting to relieve tired limbs. Only the baby seemed content. She gurgled and laughed as she lifted an outstretched hand towards the house. It was a futile attempt at touching it. She only grasped the dusty, windblown countryside air.

'Wow!' Becky exclaimed. 'I think my mind is playing tricks on me. I mean, I knew the house was big, but now it seems enormous!'

'It does, doesn't it?' Adam smiled, pleased by his wife's reaction.

'Well, I think it's the pits!' Nerea kicked at a small stone, sending it ricocheting across the sparse gravel. She hated her father for dragging them all to this godforsaken place in the middle of nowhere. Nerea had despised the house on sight, and she loathed it with a passion now. Her father's impulsive decision to buy the stupid thing meant he had forced her to move and leave her whole life behind.

As they had travelled from Almeria to their new home, Nerea had seethed at the injustice of her situation. She ruminated on how unfair life was. Having lost not only her family home but all her lifelong friends seemed unsurmountable. Her secret boyfriend, Julián, would become a bittersweet memory. She doubted a long-distance relationship would last very long. The thought of having to start all over again filled her with dark feelings of doom tinged with high levels of anxiety.

'Cheer up, Nerea, it'll be all right once you get settled in.' Becky patted her stepdaughter's shoulder. 'Look on the bright side. You're bound to have a much bigger bedroom than in the other house.'

Nerea cast a sullen, black scowl in her stepmother's direction and refrained from replying. Adam witnessed her facial expression. 'Nerea, stop being so negative.' He picked up the baby seat and placed it in Becky's hands, before gently taking hold of his mother-in-law's elbow. 'Come on, Rose, let's go see our new home!'

Rose stared up at the house, confused by the new environment. Her face broke into a broad grin. She clapped her hands in gleeful surprise. 'Ah! Look at all those children!'

'What children, mum?' Becky said, confused yet relieved by her mother's sudden enthusiasm.

'The children in the windows, dear. Look! They're waving at us!'

The others squinted towards the house, then at each other before returning their gaze to Rose, whose enthusiastic waving unnerved them.

'Hello! Hello, little children!'

Nerea shook her head. Frustration creased her brow.

Becky shrugged, and Adam grinned.

'I guess the goalposts are moving again,' he whispered.

Since Rose had come to live with them, they had learnt almost everything they could about her debilitating disease; an illness that would rob the sufferer of her memories and steal the woman whom Becky called mother from right under her nose.

'What do you mean?'

'Well, she must be hallucinating.'

Becky's eyes filled with tears.

'Hey, come on.' Adam leaned in and gave his wife a quick peck on the lips. 'This is supposed to be a happy day. Your mum's happy. You should be too.'

Becky wiped her eyes. 'Yes, I know. You're right, it's just upsetting, that's all.'

Adam didn't want to dwell on his wife's words. He patted her arm before striding out towards the front door, leaving her behind.

'Nerea, the estate agent informed me the key is under a plant pot on the porch. Why don't you see if you can find it? You can be the first person to open the doors.'

Nerea sighed to express the banality of the entire situation. She rolled her eyes heavenwards towards the nebulous clouds that crept across the sky. They enshrouded the house with a cool, unnatural shadow that chilled the air. 'I'm not bloody seven years old, Dad! I couldn't care less if I'm the first person to open the stupid doors or not!'

'Stop swearing. There's no need for it,' Adam snapped; annoyed by her lack of enthusiasm.

Despite her complaining, Nerea obeyed. She tilted the dusty, cracked receptacles one after another. Powdery soil spilt onto the flimsy, weatherworn woodwork of the rickety, old porch. Each pot housed withered, old, spindly brown plants, now well dead. 'How odd... These plants look like they've been dead for years, but six months ago, they were thriving. Why would the entire area still be flourishing yet these have been left to die?'

Adam frowned. 'I don't know. Maybe the land has an irrigation system, and these plants aren't part of it. I doubt this sunshine would take long to fry a few plants.'

Becky's eyes fell on a cockeyed, weather-worn sign that hung askew on the wall. She had no recollection of seeing it there on their previous visit, but presumed she had been too stressed about the whereabouts of her mother to notice it. She angled her head, attempting to read the peeling lettering. 'Manicomio, `La Esperanza´. What does that mean, Adam?'

Her husband adopted the same stance as Becky. He cocked his head to one side, trying to read the faded sign, then shrugged and shook his head. Turning to his daughter, he failed to notice she had frozen. The search for the key was forgotten. 'Nerea, you're the one who knows Spanish. What does it mean?'

Nerea stood up with painstaking slowness, turned her head towards the sign and squinted at the faded lettering. 'Oh, for fuck's sake!' She placed one hand on her hip and the other holding her forehead.

'Language, Nerea! And stop being a Drama Queen. Just tell us what it means!' Adam snapped.

'Well, now, let's see.' Sarcasm laced his daughter's every word. 'These two words here, "La Esperanza",' Nerea jabbed the sign with an angry finger like a schoolteacher having a bad day. 'They mean "Hope."'

'Hope,' Rose's thin voice repeated. It echoed around the drafty, weather-beaten porch.

Becky's face broke into a smile. 'That's nice, let's HOPE we will all be happy here!'

Adam groaned. 'Oh, Becky! That's terrible!' he gave her a playful push and grinned as she chuckled.

Nerea sighed but held her tongue, forcing herself not to tell them to stop acting like lovesick teenagers. Instead, she waited for them to stop flirting before continuing. 'And this word here,' she stabbed the word "Manicomio" repeatedly. 'This means mental asylum!'

The adults' laughter came to an abrupt halt.

Nerea revelled in their discomfort until she noticed the slowly building wind. It whipped up the discarded powdery soil and blew it over their feet as though it were trying to bury them; encase them forever on the property.

Becky stared at the weatherworn sign, unable to pull her eyes away from the peeling lettering. 'You what?' Her words were almost inaudible.

'Are you sure?' Adam's eyes narrowed. 'If you're messing with us, Nerea, it's not funny!'

'No, papa, I'm not messing with you. You've bought yourself a bloody mental hospital!'

'I swear that sign wasn't here when we came.' Becky squinted at the placard; her mind racing, viewing the house with fresh eyes, assessing it from a different perspective. 'I remember the ugly doorknocker. Urgh!' an involuntary shiver riddled through her body. Her index finger prodded it. 'That's got to go!'

Momentarily paralysed, Nerea stared at the gargoyle's face. She swore it had curled into a snarl at Becky's touch. The teenager tried to convince herself otherwise by stamping the soil from her shoes. She bent down to upend another crumbling plant pot. From her crouched position, she held up a rusty, old object.

'Here it is. The key to your crummy domain!' She sauntered towards her father, waggling it in his face.

He ignored her sarcasm and snatched it from her grasp. 'Okay, Nerea, open the door.'

'No way! I don't want to. Especially not now. Who knows what's inside?!'

'Oh, for God's sake, you've been in there before. You know what it's like. Just turn the bloody key!' Adam barked, annoyed with himself for coming down to his daughter's level by using profanity.

Nerea clicked her tongue, then fumbled with the cumbersome object. She thrust it into the lock, like she was violating the opening, but found she needed both hands to turn it. When the oxidised mechanism clicked open, Nerea pushed the heavy wooden doors open on their creaky old hinges.

The house groaned as though it were stretching its limbs after a long confinement; glad to have been set free from years of incarceration. A rancid, malodorous smell invaded their nostrils, forcing them all to reel back in abhorrence.

'Fuck!' Nerea wafted her hand under her nose. 'What the hell is that?'

'Don't swear, Nerea,' her dad admonished. 'That's beneath you!'

'Jesus! It stinks!' His daughter glared with defiance in Adam's direction.

Adam ignored her truculent remark. The acrid funk dissipated, as though the rush of fresh air from the strengthening wind had cleansed the old building. But it made little sense to Adam. When they had visited six months ago, the house was airy, bright, and lived in. How was it possible to have such an overpowering stench of decay? It appeared the property had been abandoned for years, not months. He didn't understand it.

'Okay, everybody inside.' He tried to sound jovial, yet his confusion regarding the unexpected situation meant he didn't quite pull it off. He held out a hand, ushering them inside.

Becky stepped over the threshold and scanned the interior of their new home with confusion. She knew the Dutch couple would have taken their belongings, but, like Adam, she struggled to understand why the house was so different. The elegance of the huge hallway and sweeping staircase appeared shallow and lifeless. Every vestige of vitality within the house had disappeared with the previous owners. A deep sense of disillusion and depression overcame Becky as if the building was emitting its feelings upon her. She couldn't shake the sinking sensation all was not right. Had they made the biggest mistake of their lives by buying this property?

Adam tried a light switch and a yellow hue from a single lightbulb painted a faint glow on the hall floor. 'Ah, good. The estate agent said he'd make sure he connected the electric, gas, and water supplies before we arrived.'

'Big wow!' Nerea mumbled.

Adam ignored her. 'First things first. A nice cup of tea. Follow me. Everyone into the kitchen!' He pointed towards the same corridor they had first traversed when they had been searching for Rose six months ago. He strode away, marching like a sergeant major. If he had expected his wife and daughter to follow suit, emulating the same amount of enthusiasm as he had, he was to be gravely disappointed. They stood in the hallway, rooted to the spot like recalcitrant toddlers being told it was bedtime, unwilling to drag their feet in his wake.

Adam's forced attempt at joviality wasn't lost on Becky. She wondered if he was also having second thoughts. The house seemed to be… how could she describe it? Tense, as though it was waiting for something horrible to happen. She kept her feelings to herself.

Nerea emitted yet another exasperated sigh.

Becky turned to her. 'Why don't you go explore? You can have the first pick of the bedrooms. It looks like you'll have plenty of choices.'

Her stepdaughter glanced in Becky's direction, eyeing her with suspicion, trying to read her mood. Nerea wondered if her stepmother had the same sick sense of doom she was experiencing. She wanted to open up and share her emotions, but their strained relationship lacked the intimacy needed to express her worries and fears.

'Okay...' Nerea dragged out the word hinting at her begrudging acceptance and ambled towards the staircase.

'Be careful!' Becky shouted after her. 'We don't know if this place is safe!'

Nerea ignored her and climbed the stairs as though she were on her way to the gallows, her heavy steps resounding around the open hallway.

From the hallway, Becky watched her stepdaughter trudging up the stairs; then she swung her head around to monitor Adam as he marched further down the corridor, swinging the baby carrier and leading the way to the vast kitchen. Rose followed behind him, the momentum of the baby seat in Adam's hand acting as a stimulant. Rose was never happier than when, under constant supervision, she could hold Melissa in her arms and talk to her.

Becky decided not to follow them. She couldn't explain it, but she needed to be alone, to have the chance to discover at least one room of the immense building on her own. To her right, she saw two heavy wooden doors. They stood a few inches apart as though they had argued and refused to be seen together. She wandered towards them. A harsh push opened them further, and Becky took one small step into a giant-sized living room. Old pieces of furniture, thick with dirt and grime, lay dotted about the room. Some still retained their dust covers, now a dirty grey from the years of accumulated powdery ashes lying on top. They reminded Becky of crematorium remains. She shivered involuntarily. How can there be so much dust? Had the Dutch couple never been in here? It makes little sense. She walked over to the first pair of heavy drapes, so dusty she was unsure as to their actual colour. They covered the windows, and the aged wooden shutters, maintaining a dull gloom within the room and a coldness that felt unnatural. Becky became overpowered by the sudden longing to throw the drapes open and let in the sunlight, even if she became covered in years of dirt, grime, and dust motes. The overwhelming necessity to bring some light and life into the property overrode everything else.

Becky grasped the edges of two drapes, throwing them open with a flourish. Years of dirt showered down onto her head and shoulders, but she didn't care. The moment the warmth of the Spanish sunlight seeped through the grimy windows; her positivity improved. Becky smiled, feeling revived as the sunlight warmed her skin. When she turned around to take in her surroundings, she jumped.

'ARRGH!' her hands flew to her heart. She took two involuntary steps backwards.

Her mother sat on one of the high-backed chairs. How Rose had crept inside without making a sound, Becky didn't know. Her heart continued to race as she stared at her mother, momentarily lost for words. 'Hello, mum.'

Rose smiled. A slight frown crossed her brow. 'Why am I here?'

Becky approached and bent down before her, relieved her mother was in a lucid state. 'This is our new home, mum.'

Rose gave a slow nod, but her eyes had already taken on a cloudy expression, and Becky recognised the sign. She had lost her mother again. 'Come on. Let's go find the others.'

They wandered down the corridor to find Adam pottering in the kitchen. On the heavy, old, wooden table, baby Melissa sat gurgling in her carry seat, examining her hands with an expression of sheer fascination.

Becky's trusty old kettle was already whistling on the Aga. She scanned the kitchen. A frisson of fear mingled with confusion forced her to pause. She remembered seeing a well-kept, highly polished Aga when they had first visited. This one was rusty and old. What the hell was going on?

Adam mistook her frown for confusion regarding the sudden appearance of their kettle on the stove.

'I went to the car for it,' he said. 'Let's have a cup of tea. Things always seem better after a cuppa.'

***

At the top of the stairs, Nerea ambled down the corridor, ran her hand along the bannister, then stopped. She peered downwards into the vast hallway, imagining she had stepped back in time. The teenager envisioned a vast plantation house with women in long, flowing, hooped dresses, their hair coiffured to perfection in the styles of yore. The images were so vivid their clarity surprised her.

Something moved.

At least she thought she caught movement out of the corner of her eye. Whipping her head around, Nerea glimpsed a cloudlike, rolling mist, which undulated down the corridor towards her. It dipped, folded, and swirled, contorting into a ghostly apparition of a woman. The cadaverous figure wearing a long colonial-style dress floated closer; the hem drifted a few centimetres from the floor, making the feet invisible under the folds of cloth. Her darkened eyes made Nerea shiver with fear. Her eyes bulged when the spectre's blackened mouth opened to form a perfect O. The ghost breathed in, sucking in the surrounding air.

Nerea immediately felt faint. The oxygen level plummeted to virtually non-existent. She gasped for air and grabbed the handrail, clinging to consciousness. The spectre continued to suck. The teenager felt like her very soul was being pulled from inside her. She felt her hair and clothing being yanked towards the ghostly spectre. Unable to move, she stared at the apparition through enlarged eyes. As the spirit inched towards her, Nerea tensed. Dreading the outcome, she squeezed her eyes closed, anticipating her fate.

Second, after elongated second ticked by with painful sluggishness. When she could no longer bear the silence, she snapped her eyes open. Shocked, Nerea realised she was lying on the ground in a crumpled heap. She must have fainted. The ghoulish image had disappeared. The air had returned to normal and Nerea inhaled; her screaming lungs gasping for oxygen. She shook her head. Had her eyes been playing tricks on her? Had she imagined the whole thing while she was unconscious? She put a shaky hand to her chest. Her heart was pounding as she fought to convince herself it was only a figment of her imagination. But was it? She had never fainted before. Nerea tried in vain to dismiss it and put the entire event down to tiredness. Determined, to deny the whole affair, she continued meandering down the corridor, forcing herself to act as though nothing untoward had happened. She swept her hand along the plastered walls and sang to herself. If she had turned around, she would have seen tiny orbs of light jumping out of the brickwork and hovering in the corridor, watching her as she strolled away.

Nerea's curiosity about finding the perfect bedroom got the better of her. She traversed the corridor and spun around. Bright sunlight shone through the stained-glass window. It masked the cluster of luminous, shimmering orbs which melted back inside the walls as she sauntered towards the staircase.

On impulse, the teenager pushed open the doors one by one, peeking into the many abandoned rooms. With a heightened sense of excitement, Nerea marvelled at the architecture and decoration within the walls of her new home. But she frowned at the abandoned furniture clustered together in the centre of each room. Why was it placed like that? She shivered, feeling watched by the oppressive presence of the mountains outside her window.

When she reached the eighth room, she discovered that, unlike the others, the door stood ajar. Intrigued, Nerea pushed it further open. The whiny creaking of the aged metal hinges groaned in protest. The noise unnerved her as she poked her head inside the room before advancing. Three steps in, and her skin contracted. Goosebumps peppered her forearms. The tiny hairs at the nape of her neck stood to attention as though a powerful magnet was exercising its gravitational pull. It stretched each hair towards the ceiling.

Almost unconscious of her body's actions, she rubbed her arms to relieve the sudden augmenting pain.

The room was as large as the others, but more organised. An aged rocking horse stood abandoned to one side, its mane matted and dirty, the paint chipped and scuffed. A faded chaise longue lay opposite, and six single beds, some still dressed in ancient blankets, had been pushed together under a window. Nerea inched over to the beds, the floorboards groaning in protest as she walked towards them and gingerly knelt on a dusty, thin, bare mattress. The metal springs of the skeletal bed frame squeaked and groaned, protesting under her weight as she gazed out of the window at the view.

On the perimeter of the property, the imposing mountains loomed above the house like bodyguards shielding a client. Nerea wasn't sure if they were controlling the garden or guarding it, but their presence was powerful. She studied the mound nearest the house. On its top, a few trees dotted the peak like uneven tufts of hairs on a balding man's head. And at the bottom, the gaping, black, cavernous orifice of a cave reminded her of an open mouth, screaming in pain.

Not enjoying the view, her vision dropped to the garden below. An abundance of lush, overgrown shrubs, trees and wild garden flowers littered the area, and in the centre stood an ancient stone wall. The rotting, weather-beaten woodwork with flaking paint strips held a rusty old, lopsided bucket on a worn length of rope.

Nerea stared at the scene and frowned. Something bugged her. Something was off. Again, she studied the garden. Then it hit her. Although the shrubbery was so overgrown, it appeared to have avoided branching out towards the well. Limbs bent and twisted as far from the structure as possible.

The teen gave an involuntary shiver, and hugged herself, not knowing why but feeling uncomfortable.

An icy chill spread through the room. The corners of each window now housed a thin layer of frost. It crept towards the centre like live spores, attempting an escape. Nerea monitored the trajectory, fascinated by the creeping tendrils of frost.

'Weird!' she said, her utterance echoing around the capacious room like a lone marble spinning inside an empty glass jar.

Despite being sixteen, she couldn't resist opening her mouth to breathe onto the glass. Nerea lifted her finger and scribbled her name on the frosty surface. As she finished the final letter, she heard a faint scurrying of tiny feet behind her.

Spinning around, she screamed as the bedroom door slammed shut.

Something moved.

She shifted her gaze. For a split second, she thought she glimpsed a hazy black mist sliding to obscurity behind the huge, old, wooden wardrobe on the back wall. Her skin became so taut, it hurt, and the hair on the back of her neck stood to attention again like a rigid army of soldiers on parade.

The primal act of self-preservation propelled her to jump off the bed and sprint towards the door. Nerea grabbed the bulbous knob and turned it. Inside, the mechanism failed to make contact. The door remained closed, sealed the room like a tomb.

Within the room, the air plummeted even further into an icy-cold frostiness. As she inhaled, her breath feathered out in front of her. Panicked, she grasped the handle in both hands, rattling and pulling until the surge of adrenalin left her exhausted.

'HELP, SOMEONE, HELP ME! I'M LOCKED IN! PAPA, AYUDAME!' she thumped on the door. Her voice reverberated around the large room, bouncing off the walls, cruelly highlighting her plight. But as her echoed words ended, she heard a vengeful, male laugh that sent chills coursing down her spine. Someone or something was playing with her, mimicking her, echoing her pleas for help with sadistic eloquence.

Nerea detected but refused to acknowledge the same black, nebulous form emerging once more from behind the wardrobe. Her stomach heaved as the fetid stench of death permeated her nostrils.

She turned her attention to the doorknob and pulled, rattled, and twisted it with frantic urgency. Her heart flipped when she heard the catch relinquish its hold and she witnessed the door separate a sliver from the frame.

Nerea emitted a weak cry of hope. She yanked on the handle, using an unknown strength, while feeling the menacing form behind her edging closer.

Her hair fell forward into her eyes. Her hands, nervous with sweat, slipped on the doorknob, but each tug inched the door open a sliver more.

She dared not risk a glance behind at the approaching presence.

The foul smell grew stronger and more repulsive as it edged ever closer. Nerea froze in fear as silent tears coursed down her cheeks. She sensed the malevolent being. It hovered inches behind her, a whisper away from touching her. The thought of deathly cold, crooked fingers fondling any part of her made her skin crawl.

Panicked, she snatched her hands away from the handle, then grabbed the edge of the door, yanking, jerking, and pulling with frantic urgency.

Behind her, a dark, wispy tendril of an arm reached out towards her. Gnarled, spindly, smoke-like fingers stretched and extended, just a breath away from pawing the ends of her hair. With one final tug, Nerea pulled the door open another inch and, by bending and twisting her body, she squeezed through, scraping her cheek on a splinter of wood. Unaware of the cut, she bolted down the corridor and shot down the stairs without a backward glance.

Inside the room, the black, amorphous form flew at an alarming rate around the bedroom, circling and circling faster and faster with pent-up rage. A deep growl of fury echoed off the walls and, with a whoosh of bone-chilling air, it darted behind the wardrobe.

One lone orb hovered by Nerea's icy imprint on the window. A second name now adorned the frosty windowpane.

A childish scrawl had spelled out 'INHARA'.

\*\*\*

Nerea sat on a rickety garden bench, replaying in her mind the event in the bedroom, unable to believe what had happened. She focused on her breathing, and when it slowed, she felt the dull, pulsing throb of her scratched cheek. Her fear had almost dissipated, yet the child inside her wanted to rush into her father's arms. She yearned for the comfort of his embrace, and his promise of fleeing the place immediately. Yet, her teenage self halted her. She couldn't turn to her father now.

Before her mother's death, Nerea's parents would read to her every night, inciting her imagination. She had loved anything mystical with fairy folk, elves, pixies, and unicorns to lull her into a blissful sleep.

With her mother's passing, the stories stopped, as Adam also grieved. They would lie together, locked in grief, enshrouded within a hug, searching for comfort in each other's arms. Night after night, Adam tried to comfort her; assuring her all was well until she cried herself to sleep.

Unfortunately, her dreams became nightmares. The once friendly fey warped into vampire bats, the elves and pixies into dark frightening shapes, and the unicorns into ferocious monsters. Nerea would wake up screaming for her father. She became afraid of the dark, imagining fierce, evil beings around every corner. Then, one day, she found an imaginary friend. At least, that was Adam's interpretation. He whisked her off to a psychologist.

Her body squirmed with unpleasant memories. The psychologist had filled her full of medication and told Adam she was using monsters to handle her grief. Nerea froze. What if she told her dad what had just happened? Would he send her off to more shrinks? She shuddered at the thought. *Maybe I've imagined it.* She tried to convince herself. *Am I that messed up?* She pictured her dad, torn between his love for her and his enthusiasm to make their new home a success. He wouldn't want her messing everything up.

Nerea knew he'd invested all his savings, so listening to a teen's rantings would only make them drift further apart. Would he even want to believe her story?

*

Becky pulled out a kitchen chair for her mother to sit down, then took an adjacent one herself and perused the kitchen from her sedentary position. 'This place is enormous, Adam.'

Her husband brought two mugs of tea to the table and grinned. 'I know!'

'It'll take lots of work.'

'Yes, but it will be worth it. There's enough space here for a dance studio, for you, a large office for me to do my writing. Hell, we could even rent out rooms to other people for other artistic purposes.'

Becky laughed at Adam's enthusiasm. His head was always in the clouds. He could dream up ideas at the drop of a hat. She shook her head and grinned at him. 'What happened to the bed-and-breakfast idea?'

'I think this will be better. If we rented out rooms to various artistic types, they could give art classes; music lessons, we might run book clubs, sculpting classes… and make it into a kind of weekend retreat.'

Becky ruminated on his suggestions. 'You know, I kind of like that idea; and I like the name too.'

'What name?'

'`The Retreat´,' she said. 'Great name! That's what we should call this place. Or better still, `Ravens' Retreat´, seeing how we've got a flock of them outside.'

Adam grinned, 'So, "Manicomio La Esperanza" isn't an option then?'

'Definitely not!' Becky scowled, her mouth twisting into a grin.

Adam rolled the words around on his tongue. "Ravens' Retreat" yeah, I like that. It makes you think of privacy, a type of sanctuary or haven.'

They smiled at one another in mutual agreement.

'Retreat,' Rose repeated. Her voice had adopted a deep, gravelly consistency, not reminiscent of her own. 'An insane asylum.' She threw back her head and an unnerving cackling filled the kitchen. 'Retreat, retreat, retreat!'

Becky stared at her mother in surprise. 'Mum?'

'Retreat, run away, hide...'

'Mum?' Becky took hold of Rose's shoulders and studied her face. The sinister voice coming from her mother's mouth sounded nothing like her. The glazed expression in her eyes completed Rose's trance-like countenance; yet, somehow, it differed from the distant, lost facial expression Becky was used to seeing.

'Flee, depart, evacuate, ESCAPE... NOW!' Rose banged two angry fists onto the worn kitchen table. Her vocalisation rose to a crescendo; only now, her utterings had adopted the consonance of a young female child.

Panicking, Becky jumped up. She placed her hands on her mother's shoulders and shook her. 'Mum, stop it. Stop it, please!'

'What the hell's the matter with her?' Nerea's voice sliced through the tension and appeared to break the spell. Rose slumped back into the kitchen chair, drained of energy. Her right hand came to the table-top, and she outlined the number eight, retracing the same continuous line in a relentless movement.

Nerea noticed it and furrowed her brow in consternation. Her mind flung her back to room number eight, where she had fought to escape. A coincidence? Or was there a link?

Becky tried to comprehend what had just happened. She recalled Adam's words about the ever-changing goalposts of her mother's illness. This outburst was new, for sure. So was the perpetual retracing of the number eight on the table. She wondered why her mother had chosen that number. Had she once lived at number eight? Was it because it was symmetrical? A never-ending swirl, which could repeat itself for all eternity? Becky didn't know, but it unnerved her.

Adam finally registered his daughter's pallid complexion bordering on white, a raw scratch down her cheek and her blood-drained face. She was leaning against the door frame, her arms folded across her chest. Her overlarge eyes emanated fear.

He edged towards her, preoccupied she might faint, and wanting to ask what had happened. But he stopped himself, deciding not to put her in the spotlight. It surprised him, though, that Rose's outburst had affected Nerea so much. He poured his daughter a drink and pulled out a chair. 'Here, sit down. It's just her illness. It's nothing to worry about.'

Nerea took the proffered mug of tea. She sat down, scrutinising Rose with a disdainful glare from behind her glass. After what had just happened to her upstairs, she had a rather different conception of the entire episode from her father. Was her step-grandmother possessed? The first voice emanating from Rose appeared to taunt them, wanting them to hide so the being– whatever it was - could find them. Yet the second, younger voice was pleading with them to flee. But who was she?

Becky's attention was on her mother, who was still outlining the number eight on the old wooden table. Rose's outburst had spooked her to her core. Was this another symptom of her illness? She had no way of confirming it. With each coming month, her mother spoke less and less as the illness progressed, and the disease ate her mind away, piece by piece.

Sometimes Rose would sleep for almost three continuous days. Whenever she regained consciousness, another motor skill would've disappeared. Left behind in dreamland, obliterated forever. Each time it occurred, it left Becky feeling bereft and with a little less of the person she identified as her mum. The last time it had happened, Rose could no longer play the piano. That had torn at Becky's heartstrings. All those years of dedication were forgotten in a heartbeat. But this was new. Strange. Becky felt perturbed by the whole situation.

Adam's voice ruptured the tense silence and brought Becky back to the present.

'How did it go upstairs, Nerea? Becky said you were looking for your new bedroom. Have you claimed one yet?'

'No.'

Nerea's sullen reply forced both her stepmother and her father to focus on the surly teenager. In an involuntary action, Becky shivered, unaware a heaviness had descended around them. Potent, static energy fell like gossamer wings, draping itself around their shoulders. It clung to the room, enshrouding them; filling them all with a pang of deep sadness they couldn't quite dispel.

An odorous stench permeated the air, forcing the family to scrunch up their noses in abhorrence.

Becky spun around in her seat, searching for the source of the foul smell. 'What the hell is that?'

Nerea stayed mum. She recognised that unearthly smell. Her hand unconsciously travelled to her swollen cheek.

Adam shook his head. He stood up and headed over to the stove, checking for a possible gas leak. He shrugged. 'I don't know, but it's putrid, whatever it is.'

Becky joined in the search, examining empty cupboards, and opening a window to allow the smell to escape.

Nerea spoke. Her enthusiastic tone contrasted with the sombre atmosphere cloaking the room. 'All the bedrooms overlook the back garden; there's a well, there, and a cave too. I think I'm gonna check it out.'

As her dad and Becky wondered at her sudden burst of enthusiasm, Nerea sat in her chair in a state of confusion; stunned by the resonance of her voice. She hated the house. The well and the cave gave her the creeps just thinking about them. She wouldn't want to investigate, either. So, what had possessed her to say such a thing? She felt she had lost control of her body for a second as if someone had spoken through her, and it scared the hell out of her.

'Okay, Nerea.' Her dad gave her a dubious smile, relieved her joviality level had improved, yet strangely unnerved at the same time by her sudden change in demeanour. 'But, later, okay? We'll explore it together. It might be dangerous. Promise me you won't wander out there on your own– especially into a cave.'

Nerea's smile disappeared in an instant. She gave her father a curt nod.

'I think the smell is dispersing. It's almost disappeared,' Becky said.

'Weird!' Adam replied, then clapped his hands together. 'Right! Becky and I'll investigate our new house and discover what we've bought!' He gave a short, embarrassed laugh.

It wasn't reciprocated by any of his impromptu audience.

'So, Nerea. I'm leaving you in charge of Rose and your sister. We won't be long.'

Before Nerea had time to protest, Adam grabbed Becky's arm. They marched out of the kitchen, holding hands, to peruse their new home.

Nerea slumped back into her chair, grabbed her phone, and started texting. Melissa slept and Rose drew a continuous number eight on the kitchen table.

Adam and Becky investigated their new abode. The downstairs had a huge kitchen and living room, plus an extensive study and two other big rooms.

An even larger staff kitchen stood at the opposite end of the house.

As the couple approached the sweeping staircase, Becky's footsteps slowed to a gentle stop. She stared in awe at the workmanship. The beautifully carved balustrades and wide, bending stairs were wondrously elegant. Although she had seen it before, she marvelled at its hidden beauty. The grandeur of bygone days lay hidden under years of dust, waiting for restoration with a fresh coat of varnish.

'Wow! This is something else! What an amazing feature! I feel like Scarlett O'Hara from Gone with the Wind.'

Grinning, Adam cupped her face in his hand and in the worst American accent ever replied: 'Frankly, Becky, I don't give a damn!'

His wife laughed and sprinted ahead up the sweeping staircase. Adam was close behind. 'I'm telling you, Becky, this was one hell of a find.' He looped his arm around her waist as they wandered towards the first closed door on the landing. 'I'm surprised the other couple didn't rent it out rather than sell it.'

Becky's brow furrowed. She wondered how to broach the subject without angering her husband. 'Huh, but... don't you think the house is odd, though?'

Adam's eyebrows knitted together. 'In what way?'

'I don't know how to explain it. It just doesn't appear to be the same house to me.'

'Well, it isn't. They took all their belongings.'

'But there's more to it than that,' Becky argued. 'For example, the furniture in the rooms is ancient. The dust cloths are so heavy with dirt and grime, it's obvious they've been there for years. How is that possible? We know people lived here only a few months ago?'

Adam frowned. 'Maybe they were renovating the house bit by bit and hadn't got around to doing those rooms yet.'

Becky returned his frown with a scowl. 'But wouldn't they at least remove the dust sheets just to check what was underneath them?' She waited for a reply that wasn't forthcoming. 'What were the rooms like when Hans walked you around?'

Adam stopped and stared into space, lost in thought. 'I know this is going to sound crazy, Becks, but I can't remember.'

'That makes no sense at all!'

Becky's words struck a chord. Why couldn't he recall the state of the rooms? He felt embarrassed by his lack of memory. How could he not remember? He turned to her and shrugged. 'Who cares? It's ours now.'

As they wandered around the ten bedrooms and three bathrooms, Becky's suspicions rose. Adam's exclamations and surprise escalated with each room they entered. *He's acting like he's never set foot here before. How is that possible?* Her thoughts made her grow quieter and even more pensive. Her spine stiffened, waiting for something unpleasant to happen. Something was off about this house. It just didn't sit right. She could feel it.

'What is it with this place and the bloody furniture?' she asked as they walked back down the stairs.

'How do you mean?'

'It's all higgledy-piggledy. Everything seems out of place. Chairs are back to front; pictures are facing the wall or hung at precarious angles. Look!' Becky pointed to the nearest picture frame to prove her point.

'Apart from the biggest pieces, like the wardrobes and the dresser in the dining room, it's all pushed together in the centre of each room, making a sort of focal point. Why is that?'

Adam shrugged. 'I don't know, but yeah, I noticed that, too. I think squatters could've caused it. Did you see the graffiti-decked walls in some rooms?' He didn't add that he also didn't remember seeing it on his previous visit. 'Maybe the house had squatters. They could've ransacked it in the interim between the Dutch couple leaving and us arriving.'

Becky held her tongue. *If that were true*, she thought, *wouldn't the squatters have removed the dust sheets? Wouldn't they have searched through everything looking for something to sell?*

'Or the housing inspectors could've moved the furniture to check the floorboards,' Adam continued. 'Who knows? And who cares! It's ours now. We can put everything back to normal and decorate it however we like.'

Becky pondered over his words. *Back to normal. What the hell is that supposed to mean? Nothing appears to be ordinary in this cavernous, old building.*

She followed him out of the bedroom and along the corridor, where they found a thin flight of winding stairs leading up into the vast expanse of attic space. A third of the space held a mountain of dusty boxes crying out to be explored. Ancient, discarded furniture in various states of disrepair languished in untidy piles. A rocking chair, crutches, wheelchairs, peeling paintings in ornate frames and dusty old trunks filled the floor space. Several smudged skylights allowed thin beams of natural light to enter the open space. The large window framed the contrast between the thriving garden and the barren landscape in the distance.

'This would make a fantastic artist's studio,' Adam said. He spun around, imagining easels, paints, and students taking master's classes.

Becky was about to reply when a loud BANG reverberated up the stairs.

They both jolted.

Becky reached out to grasp Adam's forearms, grabbing hold as though they were lifelines for her survival.

'What was that?' she whispered, searching his eyes for an answer.

Adam peered at his wife. Her pupils had enlarged with fear. Her stare penetrated his soul as she searched his face for an explanation he couldn't provide.

'It's a door slamming closed downstairs,' he said. 'Nothing more sinister than that. Maybe there's a window open somewhere.'

Becky gave a noncommittal nod, but wondered how it was possible. They had checked every individual room, and she hadn't seen a single open window.

***

Get it here: https://mybook.to/RavensRetreat

About the author:

In a past life… okay, when she was younger, Michele was a dancer, magician and fire-eater, who toured the world for over twenty years in theatre, musicals and circus. When she retired from entertainment, she went back to school and earned a First-Class Honours Degree in Modern Languages, (English and Spanish). She also studied for a Master's in High School English Teaching and is the owner of an English Language School in Spain.

During her years in entertainment, she appeared in the Guinness Book of Records for being part of the world's largest Human mobile. She has rubbed shoulders with Sting, Chris de Burgh, David Copperfield, Claudia Schiffer and Maurice Gibb from the Bee Gees. She has worked as a knife thrower's assistant, assisted a midget in his balancing act and has also taken part in the finale of a Scorpions concert.

Michele currently lives in Spain with her Spanish husband, Randy, a dog and two cats, and is an English teacher. She enjoys teaching and prepares students for the prestigious Cambridge English Examinations. There is a lot of laughter in her classroom and she feels the children keep her young. (And sometimes give her inspiration for her novels.)

She is concerned about climate change. In particular, the abundance of plastic pollution, and she hates the way man-unkind treats the other species which inhabit this beautiful planet that we are slowly destroying. She lives in the countryside with views of the sea and likes nothing better than to sit on the terrace at the end of the day, gaze up at the stars and contemplate.

You can contact the author/followed at:

https://www.facebook.com/michele.e.northwoodauthor

Twitter: @northwood_e

https://www.pinterest.es/nextchapterpub/pinterest-board-michele-e-northwood/fishnets-in-the-far-east-a-dancer-s-diary-in-korea/

OTHER BOOKS BY THE AUTHOR:

Fishnets in the Far East. (Memoir) http://mybook.to/fishnets

Fishnets and Fire-eating (Memoir) https://www.amazon.com/-/es/dp/B08LBT2LKG

Fishnets and Fleeting Contracts (Memoir) coming in 2024

The Circus Affair (Romantic crime) http://mybook.to/circusaffair

Ravens' Retreat (A paranormal Horror novel).
https://mybook.to/RavensRetreat

An Education for Emma (Romantic comedy)
https://mybook.to/SayYesToEverything

Say Yes to Everything (A comical Christmas Romance)
https://mybook.to/SayYesToEverything

A Cozy Mystery series: coming out in 2024

Summer Season at Sandy Coves: Bk 1. Kitchen thefts and the Vengeance Club.

Summer Season at Sandy Coves: Bk 2. Murder at the Manor.

Summer Season at Sandy Coves: Bk 3. Hubble Bubble Poison Trouble.


AUDIOBOOKS

Fishnets in the Far East https://books2read.com/u/mqwpWe

The Circus Affair. http://mybook.to/circusaffair

Thank you for taking the time to read `The Forest of Forgotten Time.´ If you enjoyed it, please consider telling your friends as word of mouth is an author's best friend.

I would love it if you could post a star rating or a brief review. Every single one is of huge importance to an author. They make such a difference to a writer's success.

If you would like to receive news of any new releases, book discounts, freebies, competitions or giveaways, please contact Michele at michelenorthwood@gmail.com I promise not to inundate your inbox!

Printed in Great Britain
by Amazon